JEVIC
AND THE
STONE

LISA POPP

~ DEDICATION ~

To Thom, my better half, for loving my kind of crazy.
To Heather, for believing in me until I did too.
To Christina, who is braver than she believes.
To Scott, for the hero I see in you.
To Brent, for being exactly who you are.

~ CONTENTS ~

~ INTRODUCTION ~

The Sidhe were supernaturally-gifted people who long ago traveled to Ireland upon four sailing ships from four small islands to the north. On each vessel, they carried one sacred treasure–a stone, a sword, a spear, and a cauldron. These seemingly ordinary objects possessed mystical powers beyond anything mankind had ever known, prompting the people there to refer to these strangers as the Tribe of the Gods.

These superior beings were so determined to live among men that they burned their ships upon arrival. But the people of the island were not so sure about the strangers. While many feared the Sidhe's power, others craved it, and great battles were fought as they tried to find their place among men. Eventually, they settled beneath the green hills and concealed their new home from the world above with a veil of magic. Occasionally, one or two would be seen on the surface stealing a glimpse of the precious night sky. So, to avoid further conflict in the realm of man, they used their magic to make themselves smaller. Some changed their appearance altogether. People were so easy to fool that the Sidhe never expected thieves would be clever enough to slip through the veil and rob them of their treasures.

Instantly, the Sidhe were divided. Half would have destroyed all of mankind for that heinous offense, but the others refused to punish all for the sins of a few. A thousand years later, humanity has all but forgotten the people of the hills, but the Sidhe have forgotten nothing.

1 ~ WISHES AND DREAMS ~

The flames of ninety candles danced in Alicia's eyes as she made her wish. It was the very same wish she'd made on every birthday, every shooting star, and every coin tossed into a fountain for the past fifteen years. There was only one thing Alicia O'Connor wanted from this life—for Jevic to be strong enough, smart enough, and brave enough to survive whatever this world would soon ask of him.

Across the table sat her great-grandson, Jevic, whose thoughts were haunted by a conversation overheard between his parents. He'd never worried about his grandmother's age before. Could they be right? Might this be Alicia's last birthday?

He forced a wedge of chocolate cake past the lump in his throat, and as the fork rang against his empty plate, the birthday girl rose to her feet. Without a word, he lifted her cane from a peg on the wall and swung the kitchen door open wide.

Although they'd been taking these walks together for as long as Jevic could remember, the concern on his mother's face prompted his reassurance that they'd be back soon. Alicia had taught him nearly everything he knew about wild places and wild things. She always seemed to be happiest when they were out in the woods. But today she leaned heavily on his arm when they stopped to rest beneath one enormous old tree. Jevic stared up into the branches of the humbling giant as he waited for her to catch her breath.

"Can you see 'em, Jev?" Alicia's gentle voice asked.

"It's magnificent," he replied.

"Indeed. But can you see them?" she emphasized.

"See them?"

"The faces," she whispered excitedly.

"What faces?" he asked.

"They're in the trees, Jev. There, and there, and over there." Alicia pointed in every direction.

He saw trees everywhere but only Alicia's face, which was glowing with anticipation.

"N-no," he answered hesitantly. He'd never question anything Alicia told him, but she was ninety and maybe just a little confused.

Seemingly aware of his thoughts, she assured with lucid confidence, "When it's time, you will." The distinct finality in her tone brought an immediate end to the conversation, leaving Jevic confused as well as curious.

Alicia's favorite tree was a dogwood beside the West Brook. She took her usual seat upon the lowest branch and pulled a pipe from the pocket of her sweater. It had a black onyx stem and a briar bowl emblazoned with the O'Connor family crest, a lone oak tree. Clenching the stump firmly in her teeth, she set a match to it, and the familiar scent of cherry tobacco instantly filled the air.

It had been her husband Corbin's pipe, passed down to the first son of the O'Connor family for generations. During the few precious years they had together, Corbin would enjoy an occasional smoke of that very same tobacco. Some seventy years later, the aroma could still bring him back to her in vivid memories.

Jevic quietly watched the plumes roll out over the stream and fade away. Yes, he knew smoking was bad for her health. He also knew better than to deny her the pleasure she got from that old pipe. After all, she only smoked it on special occasions and only with him. It was one of their secrets. But his grandmother had one secret she'd never shared, not even with Jevic.

Alicia broke the silence around them with a whisper, "Do you feel that, Jev? It's the magic of tween. These few precious minutes before day turns to night are truly enchanting." With a faraway look in her eyes, she asked again, "Do you feel it?"

"I sure do, Alicia." And Jevic truly did feel something, but then he always did when they were together. The incredible bond between them had undoubtedly been a catalyst for his remarkable maturity at fifteen.

He called her by her first name because she would have it no other way. Alicia meant "truthful one," which he thought suited her perfectly. His own name had come from Jevin, a Celtic word meaning young warrior, and Victor, meaning victorious. He liked his name but wondered if it actually suited him. He'd only been in one fight, in the second grade, and the black eye he'd come home with didn't exactly scream victorious.

When the last wisp of smoke had drifted from her bowl, Alicia tapped the pipe gently on the branch beneath them. The ashes spilled onto the water with a hiss as her eyes closed, and she lifted her face toward the final rays of sunshine filtering through the trees.

"Life is a grand journey," she said softly, "but it can't last forever."

Those words triggered a sinking feeling in Jevic's stomach, and there was an awkward stretch of silence. Then Alicia took Jevic's hand and gave it a squeeze, like she always did when it was time to go back.

The next day, Jevic couldn't stop wondering about the things his grandmother had said. He tried not to think about the "life can't last forever" stuff or why she felt the need to tell him such a thing. It was the idea of faces in the trees that really puzzled him.

He grabbed an apple from the bowl on the kitchen counter.

And while his mind struggled to make sense of things from the day before, his feet carried him down a slope in the woods to the little valley where the East Creek twisted through. As he approached Apple Rock, his pace quickened. He was five when he discovered the apple tree growing over top of a large, gray boulder. One of its lower limbs reached way out over the creek. That was Jevic's spot. There was little he hadn't thought about while sitting in that tree.

After he'd finished his apple, he used a stick to poke several holes in the muddy bank. Then, as he dropped a seed from the core into each hole and gave it a little pat, he smiled with satisfaction at dozens of apple trees of varying heights growing along the creek.

Jevic climbed onto his branch and had just gotten comfortable when several crows on the opposite side of the stream began to make an awful racket. Crows aren't the most likeable birds, but they can sound an alert that would put any good watchdog to shame. So, he decided to see what all the fuss was about.

From behind the stone wall at the crest of the hill, Jevic scanned the fern-covered slope on the other side. The air was absolutely still, yet one feathery leaf danced from side to side. Then, closer to the center of the ferns a second leaf moved, and a third.

It was probably just a chipmunk, but Jevic hopped over the wall to have a look anyway. As he approached, whatever had been causing the ferns to move stopped. Jevic stopped too. Except for his eyes, he was perfectly still.

A minute or two passed before he brushed the ferns aside to see what might be hiding there. But all he found was a baseball-sized rock. It was the perfect size to throw at the crows, which were still making that unjustified racket. He picked it up. His arm was back over his shoulder. His eyes were fixed on the branch beneath the nastiest noisemaker, but something made him stop. The rock felt strange. Although it was almost perfectly round, it was rough. Most rocks that round are pretty smooth. He lowered his hand to take a closer look. The color was unusual too, completely black except for a fine line of gold that ran through its center.

He wondered if it was worth anything. Probably fool's gold, but it was still pretty cool. He tossed it into the air a few times, and then slipped it into the pocket of his jeans.

Later that night, as Jevic sat on the edge of his bed examining his find, a strange feeling began to grow in the pit of his stomach. He decided it must be pangs of hunger and took the rock down to the kitchen while he looked for a snack.

The gold streak shimmered in the moonlight that flooded through the windows, and Jevic couldn't stop wondering if there was more gold inside. What if it was real? He rolled the rock around in his hand. He tossed it gently into the air and caught it several times.

A few years ago, his class had taken a trip to the Adirondack Mountains, a couple hours' drive from where he lived in upstate New York. Every kid got to choose a geode from a big barrel there. They were rough and round like this on the outside. But when they cut them open with a wet saw, there were amazing crystal formations on the inside. Maybe this one was filled with gold.

Jevic grabbed a hammer from the kitchen drawer and a towel from the counter by the sink. He folded the towel in half on the table and set the rock down in the center of it.

"Let's see what you're really made of," he whispered, lifting the hammer into the air with one hand as he flipped the towel over top of the rock with the other. A sudden, searing pain in his finger caused Jevic to pull his hand back, and at that very same moment he saw something move beneath the towel.

Blood welled up instantly on his fingertip. In the second it took to grab a napkin from the basket on the table, a red stream had run into his palm. But as he wrapped the paper napkin tightly around the wound, he never took his eyes off of the towel on the table.

After replaying the scene in his head a few times, he cautiously peeled the towel back to uncover the rock, sat down in a chair, and stared at it. There was a bump on the top he hadn't noticed before. Grabbing the towel by a corner, he dragged it to where the moonlight could hit the dark stone upon it directly. That's when he noticed an eye staring back at him.

"Holy crap!" Jevic choked.

His grip tightened on the handle of the hammer. The chair fell to the floor behind him as he scrambled to his feet. His heart pounded. If only he could reach the light switch on the wall behind him. Should he call for help? Maybe he was dreaming. He clenched his left hand into a fist and the blood-soaked napkin squished around his finger. It sure didn't feel like a dream. As Jevic straddled the thin line between reason and panic, the rock on the table spoke to him.

"You can see me now, can't you?"

Jevic's eyes opened wider, and an icy chill rolled down his spine. He took a step back and lifted the hammer into the air like a fly swatter.

The rock's eye focused directly on the young man's face as it asked again, "Can you see me?"

Jevic answered, "Yes," so softly he barely heard himself.

This is just a dream, he reasoned, and then his confused mind was reeling with options. Pick that damn thing up, and throw it out into the woods where you found it. No, smash it! Smash it!

His hand tightened around the hammer, and his heartbeat boomed like thunder in his ears. Smash it! His thoughts screamed.

As if that thing on the table knew exactly what he was thinking, the eye rolled to focus on the hammer.

What are you waiting for? Smash that thing! Jevic's head demanded. He lifted the hammer a little higher.

"No!" the voice from the table begged. "I mean you no harm. Allow me to explain," the voice from the table pleaded.

Jevic's nod was barely detectable but clearly understood, for the rock creature began to move. The young man watched in total disbelief as the eye winked and the head it was a part of lifted up from the round surface. Two arms emerged next, rising out of and peeling away, fingertip to shoulder from the dark sphere. With the flick of a tiny wrist, the gold vein became a shimmering sword. Then, the strange, dark mass rolled toward the edge of the table in Jevic's direction where the rest of it emerged, like a child from a somersault. Landing square on his feet was a tiny man dressed all in black.

He looked like a little human, scaled down to the size of an action figure. His head rocked slowly from side to side as his arms stretched into the air, and the moonlight flowed smoothly down the golden blade in his right hand.

Jevic really needed someone else to see this. He opened his mouth to call for his dad, but no sound came out. That happens sometimes when you're having a nightmare. That's what this was.

"That's much better," the little guy said.

Jevic drew a much needed breath and asked, "What are you?"

"A friend."

"Some friend," Jevic scoffed as he waved his bloody finger in the air.

"You were about to smash me," the stranger argued.

Jevic glanced at the hammer hanging in the air above the little guy's head but wasn't ready to lower it yet.

"My apologies," said the stranger in a somewhat sympathetic tone. "That was not the way I wanted to introduce myself. Nevertheless, you have gained much for the little blood you've lost." He strode confidently to the edge of the table and lifted the sword to eye level.

Jevic's grip tightened as the stranger's gloved hand ran slowly down the length of his blade. "That was amazing!" he commented.

"The way you changed?" Jevic asked.

"No, I do that all of the time," the small stranger dismissed as he returned his sword to its scabbard. "It's the way you've changed that's so amazing. You're a Seer now. You've been given the Gift of Sight through that wound on your finger."

Then he brushed the straight, black hair away from his face,

7

and for the first time, Jevic got a good look at his dark eyes.

"When a weapon forged in my realm draws the blood of a human, the rare Gift of Sight is bestowed to the wounded one. This is why you can see me now." The little guy's pace quickened with excitement for the young human as he added, "You should be able see the entire dimension of spirit that mingles invisibly with the mortal world. Jevic, you will understand secrets of the earth that other humans can only dismiss as "magic" or "figments of their imagination.""

"You're a spirit?" Jevic asked, trying to grasp some understanding of what was happening.

The hint of a smile softened the small stranger's face. "Yes, I am a spirit of the earth," he acknowledged. "In this form, we're known as fairies and elves, but we can take many shapes."

"No kidding?" Jevic's cheeky reply softened the stranger's face for a second time. Then he asked, "Where do you live, by the creek?"

"We are everywhere. You have the Sight now…you will see."

Don't fall for this crap. You're dreaming, Jevic's reason warned. But his curiosity outweighed all reason, and he asked, "What's your name?"

"Aaron," the little fellow promptly replied. Then his gaze focused briefly on the hammer, and he smiled.

Jevic lowered his weapon to the table where it was still easily within reach as he responded, "My name is…"

"Jevic, I know who you are," Aaron interrupted, and that's when Jevic recognized Aaron's voice. It was the voice, that voice he'd never been able to explain. Why hadn't he recognized it sooner?

"You have great purpose in this life, Jevic O'Connor. And it is my honor to protect you," Aaron said, bowing slightly at the waist.

"What?" Jevic chuckled, like someone losing all sense of reality. He frantically ran his hands through his hair, giving a little tug in hope it would jerk him back to consciousness.

Seemingly desperate to help him understand, Aaron said, "It's almost time..." and then the click of a switch flooded the kitchen with light.

"Jev, what are you doing up?" his mom asked from the doorway behind him.

He turned in her direction for only an instant, but that was long enough. Aaron had vanished. Jevic snatched the empty dish towel from the table giving it a shake. He struggled to scan the room as his eyes adjusted to the light. He dropped to his knees and crawled beneath the table checking the seat of each chair. But there was no sign of the tiny man or the mysterious rock anywhere.

"Are you all right?" his mother asked.

"It's gone!" he panicked.

"What did you lose?" she calmly asked.

"My rock, that round, black rock I found by the creek."

"Maybe your father tossed it out into the yard."

"No!" Jevic snapped. Then, he took a deep breath and tried to explain. "It was just here. That was no ordinary rock, Mom..." he began, but he stopped abruptly. He couldn't tell her what had happened. There was no way she'd believe any of it. Even he didn't believe it.

Jevic pulled himself up off of the floor and shook his head. He really didn't believe it. Stuff like this only happens in movies and dreams. If he could just wrap this one up, he can put the whole thing behind him when he opens his eyes in the morning.

He turned toward his mom and threw his hands into the air. "It was just a stupid rock," he said as the blood-soaked napkin slipped off of his finger and fell to the floor.

"You're hurt!" she cried. She grabbed his hand, twisting it in one direction and then the other, but there was no trace of a wound anywhere. "Where did all of that blood come from?" his mother demanded.

"I cut my finger," Jevic answered vacantly, not at all sure if any of this was really happening.

His mom scooped up the napkin and dropped it uncertainly

into the trash. "How could a cut bleed that much and then magically disappear?" she wondered aloud.

As Jevic's eyes swept through the room one more time, he whispered, "It was like magic."

2 ~ SUPERHEROES ~

After a sleepless night, Jevic stood in the kitchen staring down at the blood stained napkin in the trash. For the hundredth time, he relived what had happened the night before. It must have been real, he reasoned.

"Morning, Jev," his mother greeted groggily. She patted the top of his head as she shuffled past in her slippers. "How's your finger?"

"Fine," he answered. "I still can't see where the cut was. Maybe I have superhero powers or something." He grinned and snatched a banana from the bunch on the counter.

His mom was standing in front of the coffee pot scooping Morning Breakfast Blend into the filter. "I sure hope so," she told him. "The world could always use another hero."

"Mom?"

"Yeah, Jev."

"Did you ever have anything weird happen to you that you couldn't explain?"

She stared blankly out the window into the woods for a few seconds before answering. "I thought I saw a UFO once. Trust me, that's not something you want to go around telling people." She gave him a wink. "Your father still gives me a hard time about it. I couldn't sleep for weeks. I'd sit up at night watching the sky, waiting for it to come back. Thought if I could just take a picture, everyone would believe me. But I never saw it again. I suppose it could have been a plane or my eyes were playing tricks on me."

"Or your imagination?" Jevic suggested.

She smiled. "Yes. It may have been my imagination. Honestly, who knows what's real and what we conjure up in our own heads." She looked up at the clock on the wall and added, "The bus will be here in about two minutes. You'd better get going."

Jevic stuffed the second half of the banana into his mouth and threw his backpack over his shoulder.

"Did something weird happen that you want to talk about?" she asked.

He stared at the napkin sitting boldly on top of the trash. "No. I was just curious," he mumbled. Then he tossed his peel on top of the napkin and closed the lid. "Love ya, Mom," he added with a quick peck on her cheek.

A lime green bike was his transportation down the seven hundred foot gravel driveway. He skidded to a stop on the bridge over the East Creek to watch the water and take a few deep breaths of morning air. This would be a perfect day to spend lying on my back at Apple Rock, he thought. Wonder if I could talk Mom into letting me have a day off. Then the bus hissed its brakes at his stop. Too late, he told himself. He peddled hard around the last turn, hopped off the bike while it was still moving, and let it sail in the tall grass where it flopped onto its side.

The bus ride was about an hour long, but he sat with his best friend, Brent Thomas, which made it seem shorter. Brent lived a mile down the road and was the youngest of four kids. His sisters and brother were all older and out of the house, making him somewhat of an only child, like Jevic. However, having grown up with a house full of kids seven to twelve years older than he, Brent was more mature than most guys their age.

Straight, ash blonde hair, cut in a casual California style, was kind of Brent's trade mark. While most kids were wearing their hair short, he kept his long. Being different didn't bother him, not much did. With little effort, he was a great student. He had a fantastic sense of humor, and he knew he was a good guy. So unlike most teenagers, Brent honestly didn't care what anyone else thought, except for Jevic. The two of them were closer than most brothers.

"Morn'in," Brent said, plunking down in the seat beside him. It took about two seconds to notice his best bud was looking a bit out of sorts. "Rough night?" he asked.

"Might say that," Jevic answered.

"Up all night playing video games?" Brent surmised.

"No. I just had trouble sleeping."

"Wasn't a girl, was it?" Brent chuckled.

Jevic liked girls, and they loved him. But he hadn't met one interesting enough to pursue yet. He didn't see any sense in dating just to say he was dating. If there was supposed to be someone special for everyone, he'd rather wait for that special someone. Besides, there was plenty of other stuff he wanted to do in the meantime.

Jevic pretended to laugh and changed the subject. "Want to come to my house tomorrow to work on the Social Studies project that's due Monday?"

"Jeez, I forgot all about that," Brent admitted. "Sure. It won't take all day, right? Maybe we can work on that cabin we've been talking about. If we get it built by the end of the school year, we can sleep in it this summer."

Perking up a little, Jevic agreed, "That sounds cool! I think my dad has some lumber scraps in the shed he's been saving for us."

"Hey, did you hear about old Mr. Stewart?" Brent whispered discretely, his expression taking on a solemn quality.

"The one who runs the hardware store?" Jevic asked.

Brent nodded. "He was late getting home for supper Wednesday night. And when his wife went looking for him at the store, she found him dead on the floor behind the counter."

"Was it a robbery?" he asked.

"Nope, looks like a heart attack," Brent replied.

"How old was he?"

"My mom said he was eighty-one." Brent shook his head. "I liked that guy. Always gave me lollipops when I went in there, no matter how big I got."

"Yeah, me too," Jevic said softly. Although he felt bad about Mr. Stewart, it was more disturbing that someone younger than Alicia had died so suddenly. He'd never lost anyone close to him. It would be awful. In fact, it was too horrible to think about. Hoping to change the subject again, he asked, "Are you going to bring your bike with you tomorrow?"

"Sure. I'll throw it in the back of Dad's truck with all the lumber we have to contribute. Dad will be glad to get it out of the garage. How's ten o'clock sound?"

"Good," Jevic answered. Hoping to forget about poor Mr. Stewart, he started thinking about where to put the cabin. He couldn't wait. They'd talked about building a place for the two of them to hang out for years, and now it sounded like it was finally going to happen.

By fourth period, Jevic was definitely feeling his lack of sleep. Mrs. Thompson was going on and on about obtuse angles. It was all he could do to keep from dozing off.

The sun was shining into the room through the huge windows that ran along the wall to his left. Across the street, a farmer was plowing his field, and the smell of dirt wafted through the open windows. Jevic loved the smell of dirt. It reminded him of the creek.

Suddenly, he was there on his branch at Apple Rock, dangling his feet and feeling the warm sunshine on his face. Beneath him, the water gurgled past on its way to somewhere else. He pictured himself floating along with it. He passed under the bridge where the driveway crossed and spilled into a pool on the other side. It was the only place along the creek where the water rested for a while, and he enjoyed drifting there with the sun shimmering off the ripples all around him.

The eraser end of Brent's pencil jab into the middle of

Jevic's back, and he heard the teacher ask, "Am I putting you to sleep Mr. O'Connor?"

He opened his eyes to a room full of faces staring at him. "I guess so," he answered groggily.

"What?" the teacher snapped.

"I mean…no, Ma'am. It's not you; it's all those obtuse angles." He pushed himself up in his seat and tried to say something that would make the teacher stop looking at him that way. "In fact, geometry in general really puts me to sleep." There were gasps and giggles all around the room. Jevic was a pretty good student and usually only a wise guy to his friends, not to the teachers.

"I'm sorry to hear that, Mr. O'Connor," she said in a tone that didn't sound very sorry at all. "Perhaps if you spend a little more time with me during twelfth period, it would help."

"I doubt it." Jevic cringed at the words that came out of his own mouth. What was going on? He just wasn't himself.

An outburst of laughter brought color to the teacher's face, and her jaw clenched. Jevic attempted to repair the situation. "I apologize. I didn't get much sleep last night. I'm really not trying to be funny." He followed up with a feeble attempt at the charming grin he'd perfected for situations like this. Then he rubbed his hands over his face and sat up straighter in his chair.

Heather Fields, who sat to Jevic's right, was the brightest student in the class. Her parents were hippies who never left the 70's, so she was bound to stand out in the crowd a generation later. With wavy blonde hair that came down to her waist, pine-green eyes and pixie-like features, she'd probably have stood out anyway, but she acted and dressed so differently that none of that mattered. Being so darn smart on top of everything else made her nearly intolerable to the guys, and most of the girls, in their class.

When Heather politely raised her hand, anticipation dissolved the laughter in the room.

"Miss Fields," the teacher acknowledged through clenched teeth.

"There was a full moon last night," she stated as the room fell completely silent. "I didn't sleep well myself. It's a known fact that the phases of the moon have a strong influence on not only the sleep patterns of humans but on all animals, as well as on the tides, gravitational pull, growing season…"

Mrs. Thompson interrupted, "Thank you, Heather."

When the teacher turned away, Heather glanced at Jevic, who was completely surprised but grateful for the distraction.

"Thanks," he whispered.

Mrs. Thompson made no further mention of twelfth period when Jevic apologized again on his way out of the room. But as soon as they'd cleared the doorway, Brent asked, "What the heck was that?"

"What was what?" Jevic asked.

"Why was Heather sticking up for you? Is there something you forgot to tell me?"

"No. I was just as surprised as you."

"Well, she sure saved your butt. Maybe she'll tutor you and make math more interesting." Brent suggested with a slap to Jevic's back as he crossed the hall to his locker.

Sixth period was lunchtime. Jevic was always hungry and generally made sure he was one of the first people in line at the cafeteria, even if it meant running down the hall to beat the crowd. He was about to grab his tray when Heather walked up behind him with a smile.

"Hi," he said, stepping aside to let her ahead of him.

"Wide awake for lunch, I see," Heather teased.

"I have my priorities," Jevic chuckled. "Thanks again."

"You're welcome," she said. "Somebody had to save you from yourself."

Jevic couldn't help but notice that she was blushing and what a nice smile she had. He also noticed she took the vegetarian plate and an apple instead of chocolate cake.

"You like apples?" he asked.

"They're my favorite."

"Mine too."

Jevic was unsure how to end the conversation and

wondering what was keeping Brent as he mumbled, "Well, I guess I'll see you around."

"Sure." Heather smiled.

Jevic was halfway through his fish stick sandwich when Brent pulled out the chair beside him. He grabbed the red plastic bottle from the center of the table, lifted the top of his bun, and added a generous amount of ketchup on top of his tartar sauce smothered fish.

Jevic shook his head and wrinkled up his nose.

"Don't knock it till you try it," Brent argued.

Jevic shook his head. "Not a chance," he told him.

Their table had just filled up with the usual gang when Christina Evans, the most popular girl in the ninth grade class, walked up.

"Does anyone have a quarter I could borrow?" she asked sweetly.

Every guy there turned his pockets inside out. But as luck would have it, this was not a wealthy group. The best they could pool together was three nickels and a retainer. "Thanks anyway," Christina said politely as she moved on to the next table.

Seconds later they heard Robert Reilly say, "All I have is a fifty." Then, leaning his chair onto its back legs, he gave Christina a wink and said, "You'll have to earn it though."

She shot him an icy glare as she walked away.

"Just kidding, Christina," Robert taunted. "You're not worth more than a quarter anyway."

"I wish somebody would teach that jerk a lesson," Christina whispered as she reached the table with her friends.

Her face was red, but surprisingly, not as red as Brent's. He stood up with his tray in hand and kicked the back leg of Reilly's chair right out from under him. Robert probably did have a fifty in his pocket, but that didn't give him the right to mistreat a nice girl like Christina. Brent didn't have much money, but he always had right and wrong figured out. He'd also had a crush on Christina Evans since kindergarten, and until now, Jevic was the only one who'd known about it.

"Now, you're funny," Brent said, looking down at Robert lying flat on his back. When he headed for the tray return window without another word, Robert grabbed for Brent's leg, but Jevic casually pushed his chair between them as he stood up with his own tray.

"You'll be sorry, Thomas," Robert threatened.

"Doubt it!" Brent shouted back as he strolled out of the cafeteria.

Later that afternoon, as Jevic sat on the living room sofa doing homework, he peeked over the top of his science book at Alicia who was knitting in her rocking chair. Every day Alicia would knit, and everything she made was donated to the local orphanage or the church; baby blankets, scarves, hats, and mittens tied into pairs with a piece of yarn at the cuff. The church had a mitten tree at Christmastime. On it, the brightly colored yarns she favored brilliantly decorated the tree before they were given to kids who needed them.

Even the old folks' home in the next town received a box of lap blankets twice a year, just the right size for the residents to cover their legs with as they sat watching TV or playing cards.

Suddenly Jevic's thoughts were invaded by Mr. Stewart's recent demise. Intentionally turning his focus back to his homework, he put his feet up and stretched out to concentrate on his reading. Halfway through the first page, it happened. A voice, the voice, whispered, "It's almost time," into his left ear.

Jevic's head spun toward his great-grandmother on the other side of the room. "What?" he asked.

"I didn't say anything, Dear," Alicia replied.

"Did you hear that?" he quizzed.

"Hear what?"

Jevic was certain someone had just whispered directly into his ear. He hopped off of the sofa to take a look around.

"Jev, what's the matter?"

"I heard a voice," he replied.

Alicia asked, quite calmly, "Well, what did it say?"

"It's almost time!" Jevic told her. "Someone whispered right into my ear, 'It's almost time.'" Then he snatched the pillows from the sofa, gave them a shake and tossed them back in place.

"Did you recognize the voice?" Alicia asked.

Jevic had heard Aaron speak those very same words the night before, and he'd heard that same voice countless times in the past, but he didn't want to admit to any of that.

"It wasn't my imagination," he insisted. "I really did hear a voice."

"I believe you did," Alicia assured softly.

When Jevic plopped down on the sofa, his face furrowed, Alicia dropped the bright orange mitten attached to her knitting needles into her lap.

"Imagination," she echoed. "Jev, in my lifetime, I've heard voices in my head, on the wind, and in my dreams that had nothing to do with my imagination. There is much about this world that we do not know."

She stopped rocking and leaned toward him. "The spirits of the earth occasionally brush against us, even whisper into our ear. Most people quickly dismiss such things as figments of their imagination; but that's not always wise."

"What am I supposed to do, talk back like some crazy person?" Jevic asked.

Alicia's eyes sparkled. "Perhaps you're crazy if you don't."

3 ~ CHANGE ~

Jevic and Brent hiked into the woods, determined to find the perfect location for their cabin. They'd talked about building it in a tree, and Jevic wanted to show Brent a large pine he thought would be perfect.

The two teens were about the same height with the same slender build. Were it not for their hair, it would have been difficult to tell them apart as they climbed the hill with their stacks of lumber. Despite their struggle to maneuver between trees and avoid getting snagged on thorny bushes with the building materials they were carrying, it didn't take very long to reach the tree they were looking for.

"That's the one," Jevic declared, dropping his armload of boards as he nodded toward the big, old pine tree towering over them.

"That thing's huge!" Brent gasped. "There's probably a hundred times the lumber we just carried here in that thing."

"Maybe more," Jevic said.

Brent walked closer to the base of the needled giant to examine its structure. Four major limbs extend evenly in every direction from the main trunk. The symmetry was remarkable. It would take little effort to attach a level floor to a foundation like that.

Jevic gathered several fallen branches from around the tree and tossed them aside. His footsteps were cushioned by a century's worth of fallen needles that made the ground sound hollow. It felt hollow too, something he'd experienced countless times in the past, but today he was much more aware of it.

Meanwhile, Brent used stubs of broken branches like foot pegs to climb up into the tree. He stood on one of the main limbs and slapped one of the others, like the shoulder of an old friend. "We're going to be spending a lot of time together," he said softly. Then he shouted, "Jev! If you hand me the saw, I'll clear some of this dead wood out of our way."

Jevic slipped the backpack off of his shoulders and gave his friend the saw he had packed inside. Near the trunk, he noticed a large vine that had grown up into the branches. There were vines like this all over the forest. They could kill a tree off in a year or two if left unattended. When he gave it a tug, it barely moved. So he pulled harder, again and again. He gripped the vine firmly, lifted his feet right off of the ground, and tugged at it with all his might. It finally began to drop a foot or so at a time until it completely broke free. When it did, Jevic was caught by surprise. He stumbled a few steps backwards and landed on his butt.

"You ought to be dangerous when you're a few feet off of the ground," Brent laughed.

"Look who's talking," Jevic argued. "You can't even walk through the cafeteria without knocking people over in their chairs."

Brent smirked. "Yeah, I probably shouldn't have done that," he admitted. "But that guy needs somebody to knock him down a peg or two. Who does he think he is, talking to Christina like that?"

"The look on his face when he hit the floor was worth fifty bucks," Jevic chuckled. He hesitated for a couple of seconds before asking, "You do realize everyone knows how you feel about her now?"

"Yeah, her friends were giggling every time I walked by for

the rest of the day. Girls are so goofy."

Jevic wiped off the seat of his pants and was winding the vine into a pile to keep it out of their way when Brent pointed at a dead branch just above his head.

"Jev, should I cut this off too?" he asked.

Jevic shook the hair out of his face to get a clear view and was immediately taken back by what he saw. Was something strange about the way the sunlight was playing through the leaves onto the surface of the tree? He took a step to one side, but the peculiar, shadowy image was still there. Jevic raked his fingers through the curly mop on his head as he stared in utter amazement. There was a face looking back at him from the trunk of that tree just below Brent's feet. It had dark, tired eyes and a bulbous nose that twitched occasionally as the mouth below it appeared to be speaking.

He was mesmerized as the lips and cheeks moved with the fluid motion of a human face. The subtle bumps and knots of the tree he knew so well were now obvious features and character lines in a bizarrely animated face; a face that was apparently trying to communicate with him.

When the speaking motion stopped, the eyes on the tree face looked upward as if irritated by the young human in his branches.

"Jev, what do you think? Cut it or leave it?" Brent asked again.

"Leave it!" Jevic shouted without the slightest glance at the branch in question. He blinked hard a few times, but the face was still clearly visible. Was he losing his mind?

"I think we should leave the rest just as it is," he suggested. "Come take a look from here."

Brent climbed down to have a look for himself. Jevic felt much better with his friend standing safely beside him, and he was anxious to see if Brent would notice the face.

"Well?" Jevic asked.

As if the pine knew exactly what he was thinking, a wise old smile lifted the corners of the mouth.

Jevic drew a short, nervous breath and turned his gaze

toward his friend. "How does it look to you?" he asked. To his surprise, the shakiness in his voice went unnoticed.

"Pretty good, I guess," Brent answered.

"Do you see anything…unusual about it?" Jevic prodded.

"Just an extraordinary pruning job," Brent gloated.

"Yeah," Jevic replied tersely, "But do you see anything special about it?"

"What's the matter with you?" Brent asked. "It's a tree. There's nothing special about it. We're surrounded by hundreds of them."

"Well, I can kinda see a face on it," Jevic reluctantly confessed.

"Where?" Brent asked.

Jevic pointed out the features. "There's the nose, eyes and the mouth. It looks like an old man's face. Can you see it now?"

When the tree face seemed to be speaking again, Jevic got a huge lump in his throat. He was certain Brent would have to see it when it was moving like that.

"I don't see anything. Must be the way the light is hitting it, or it's just your imagination," Brent reasoned without the slightest indication of doubt.

If he was the only one who could see that thing, maybe he had completely lost his mind. Jevic's gaze was locked on the strange eyes following his every move as he reached into his backpack for a tape measure.

Brent headed back toward the tree, and Jevic didn't know how to stop him. The fact that he'd spent the majority of his life in these woods was the only small comfort he had. Every tree, rock and animal in the hundreds of acres that surrounded them was as familiar as the contents of his own bedroom. These were his woods, the safest place in his whole world. Although this was completely freaking him out, he somehow knew that nothing here would harm either of them.

There was nothing to do but closely follow Brent. Taking care not to get his feet too close to the mouth, Jevic pulled himself up into the tree where he could no longer see the face.

But he couldn't stop thinking about it either. He'd been climbing trees as long as he could remember. Never before had he felt so uneasy in one.

Although they measured the distance between limbs where the frame of the floor would rest, Jevic didn't remember any of the measurements. In fact, he could barely hear Brent reading the measurements over the sound of his own heartbeat pounding in his head.

They hopped back down to the ground, and Brent ran to measure the boards in their lumber pile. Jevic took two steps and stopped to gather the nerve to look over his shoulder at the old pine again. When he did, it was still there, and apparently, it was still trying to communicate. Since he had no control over the situation he attempted to rationalize it. What are you afraid of? It's just a tree, he thought.

"Grab the saw, will ya?" Brent yelled, "We'll have to cut six inches off of this one."

The saw was hanging from the stub of a branch on the side of the tree where Brent had left it. Jevic moved his feet before he had time to think about it. He walked back toward the tree staring boldly at the face.

I'm not afraid. What's he gonna do, chase me? He snatched the saw. Then, without a moment's consideration, he dropped to one knee between its mossy roots and stared directly into its eyes. When the mouth began to move again, he scrambled frantically to his feet and took a few brisk steps back before he stopped. His legs wobbled, and a drop of sweat rolled slowly down the side of his face. What do you want? What are you trying to say to me? Just leaf me alone, will you, he joked nervously in his head, making the situation less threatening just long enough for his instincts to take control.

"I am crazy," he whispered letting the saw fall from his hand. Then he stepped up to the tree and dropped onto his knees once more. Allowing himself no time to reconsider, Jevic quickly pressed his ear against the tree trunk, just to the left of the face.

"It's an honor to meet you, Jevic," a deep voice rumbled softly through the tree.

He recoiled, and the tree face smiled understandingly. Its eyes shimmered with compassion, and at that moment, Jevic realized there was nothing to be afraid of. He pressed his ear against the trunk for a second time.

"You don't have to be afraid," the tree reassured him. "I've watched you grow up in our woods, and I'm happy you can finally see me as the life force that I am. You have great purpose in this world, Jevic."

"Jev, what are you doing?" Brent yelled. His voice seemed distant, as if he was trying to wake him from a dream.

Jevic pulled himself slowly to his feet and backed away, unable to believe what was happening.

"Jevic? Bro, are you all right?" Brent asked.

"Yeah, I just thought I saw something again," Jevic replied blankly as he picked up the saw and carried it over to his friend.

"Are you ok?" Brent asked. "You're as white as a ghost."

"I…I'm fine. Where do ya want this thing cut?"

"That line, right there," Brent told him.

Jevic cut all of the boards where Brent had them marked, and they nailed four of them together into a frame.

"Well, I guess we're ready to nail it to the tree," Brent said.

These words roused Jevic from his dazed state, and his eyes opened wide. "Nail it?" he repeated. He looked over his shoulder at the tree as the face on it appeared to wince. "Oh, God!" he whispered under his breath.

"Let's carry it over and set it into place," Brent suggested excitedly.

Jevic's mind was churning, so was his stomach. Why was this happening to him? How could he tell his friend that this whole cabin idea was no good after all? They carried the frame over and lifted it carefully onto the branches. When Brent pulled a hammer out of his belt and a nail out of his back pocket, Jevic's mind was racing to find some way out of this predicament.

"Uhh, wait!" he stammered. "I'm not sure nailing this is such a great idea."

"What," asked Brent? "Why are you acting so weird?"

"I heard some types of nails can kill a tree. We don't want to hurt this old guy, do we?" Jevic struggled to force a smile, but the nervous, sickly expression already on his face overshadowed it.

"You're such a dork," Brent informed him. "Don't worry; I'll drive the nail so you'll be just an innocent bystander."

Jevic held his breath as the hammer rang against the nail. Each strike tied the knot in his gut a little tighter. While the nail inched its way through the board and into the living wood, Jevic closed his eyes and dropped his forehead against the tree.

"Jevic, why do you pierce my flesh?" the tree groaned.

"Stop!" Jevic yelled. "Brent, you have to stop."

He froze the hammer in mid-swing.

Desperate for any excuse that wouldn't make him look like a head case, Jevic blurted excitedly, "Let's try lashing it to the branches instead. That would support all of this weight better than a few puny nails that will bend and rust away."

Brent dropped the hammer to his side and gazed at him critically. After a few seconds, he said, "You might be right. The Swiss Family Robinson's tree house in Disneyland was tied together with rope like that. Do you have any rope?"

"Sure do," Jevic exhaled. "It's down in the shed."

"Let's go grab the rope and some more lumber," Brent suggested enthusiastically. Then he dropped the hammer near the base of the tree and started walking down the hill toward the shed.

Relieved, Jevic let his head fall back against the tree and heard the voice again. "Thank you, my friend."

A lump tightened in his throat and his eyes welled up. He lifted the hammer from the ground, hooked the claw end onto the nail head, and pried it carefully out of the wood. The wind whispered through the branches of the old pine like a sigh. Jevic slipped the nail into his pocket and wiped away a tear with the back of his hand.

As bizarre as all of this was, what he saw next as he gazed through the woods toward home changed Jevic's life forever. Every tree in the forest was looking at him, each with its own unique face. There were aged faces on tall trees and baby faces on saplings so small they were barely visible. Lovely young faces framed by curls of white bark smiled at him like school girls from a stand of birches. Without a doubt, this was the most astonishing vision he had ever seen, and he tried not to blink, fearing they would all disappear if he did. Even more than the beauty of the faces around him was the peaceful feeling that washed over him, like he was completely surrounded by friends.

As he stood there consumed by the moment, something scooted across the forest floor—something dark and about a foot high.

Jevic immediately called out, "Aaron?"

The figure darted along a straight path toward the creek, briefly visible between trees as it traveled swiftly, quietly over the hillside. Jevic sprinted through the forest after the small, dark figure intermittently visible a consistent 100 feet ahead of him. Before he knew it, he was splashing through the swampy ground beside the East Creek and then face-to-face with the tree at Apple Rock.

There weren't many things that could have stopped his pursuit of the figure he believed to be Aaron, but seeing the face of his dear friend for the first time was definitely one of them. Jevic's jaw dropped.

The apple tree's face had large, beautiful eyes and long lashes that swept upward when she smiled at him. The rich, green moss circling the base of the tree wrapped like a shawl over her shoulders and down the limb, his limb, which reached out over the running water.

Although this had always been the most beautiful tree in Jevic's world, he now stood and stared in disbelief until he could finally breathe, "Hello."

The tree face looked toward her limb, inviting him to sit on the branch he'd sat upon thousands of times before. But now

27

he took his place much more carefully than ever before and slowly leaned his head back against the trunk. He dare not even imagine what it would be like to hear his old friend speak.

"Jevic," a gentle voice sang through the tree, "It's so good to see you."

The young man blinked hard and turned to look directly into the eyes of his apple tree.

"I can't believe I can see you like this," he whispered. They had shared many of the best moments in his life together in this place. How often had he spoken to this friend whom he could trust with any secret, any problem?

As she began to speak again, he reached out to touch her cheek. When his fingers caressed the bark, he could hear her.

"I am so proud of the young man you've become," she told him.

"Why is this happening to me?" he asked. If anyone would tell him, she would.

"You've been preparing for this your whole life, Jevic," she said. "Every living thing of this world has a purpose. Mine was to be here for you as you grew. However, your destiny is much more important."

"Everyone keeps telling me that, but I don't know what you're talking about," he professed. "I'm just a kid. What can I do?"

"Even the smallest star shining between day and night can grant a wish. The world needs you now, Jevic O'Connor. It is time," the tree whispered with a smile so warm it nearly melted his heart.

"Time for what? I don't understand what I'm supposed to do. Can you tell me?" he pleaded desperately for an explanation.

She lowered her eyes and answered, "I cannot."

From behind the large rock at the base of the tree came a familiar voice. "I can take you to someone who knows," said Aaron as he stepped proudly into view.

Before another word could be exchanged, there was a rustling of leaves at the top of the hill, and Brent came running down the slope.

"What are you doing down here? he asked. "I've been looking all over the woods for you."

"I saw something run this way," Jevic began to explain. As he did, a round, black rock about the size of a baseball rolled up beside his foot. He stared at it for a moment, and then looked up at his friend.

"What was it?" Brent asked.

Something was telling him to fill his best friend in on everything strange that had happened, and something else was telling him Brent wouldn't believe him if he did. He looked over his shoulder at the apple tree's knowing smile.

"I'm not sure what it was. It ran down here, but I lost it," he twisted the truth.

Trying to retain what was left of his enthusiasm, Brent asked, "Well, are we gonna get that rope or not?"

"Sure," Jevic answered quickly, grateful that Brent apparently hadn't heard him talking. As he shifted his weight to take a step, the black rock rolled into his heel with a solid thump. He stared down at it for a second or two, unsure of whether to pick it up or to leave it behind with the hope that all of this crazy shit would just go away. His head was whirling with questions though, and if Aaron could help him find answers, he had to hang on to him.

Jevic scooped the rock from the ground. Then, although nearly overwhelmed with a sense of vulnerability as the band of gold caught his eye, he warned, "You'd better stay like that," as he slipped the rock into his pocket.

4 ~ THE CHANGER ~

Brent seemed completely unaware that the entire forest was watching them that afternoon. So Jevic tried not to stare at the incredible tree spirits as they vied for his attention or to rouse his friend's suspicion that anything was out of the ordinary. But no matter how hard he tried to ignore the obvious changes taking place to his perception of reality, the bulge in his pocket was a constant reminder. Amidst the chaos inside of his head, he somehow knew that because of that rock his life would never be the same.

Brent's dad picked him up just before dark, and Jevic knew his mother would soon be calling him for dinner. So he closed the shed door behind him and turned on the light. Trembling with excitement, he carefully removed the rock from its hiding place and held it under the murky light from the bulb overhead. He rolled it around in the palm of his hand. It was amazing that this thing that looked like a rock and felt like a rock wasn't a rock at all. The black sphere was lifeless and cool upon his skin. He saw no eye, nor the slightest resemblance to a little man's body in the shape of it now.

"We're alone," Jevic said softly. "It's safe to show yourself now."

His heart beat faster with the anticipation of seeing the

same transformation he'd witnessed two nights earlier, but nothing was happening. He switched hands and repositioned the rock in case it was upside down or something. It made no difference. The sphere sat perfectly still in the palm of his hand.

"Aaron?" he whispered, "Are you in there? It's me, Jevic." Still nothing happened.

What was wrong? Could being inside of his pocket all afternoon have killed the little man? Maybe he suffocated. Maybe he stayed like a rock too long and now there was no turning back.

"If you can't show yourself, can you at least speak to me?" he pleaded, but there was no response.

What was different the other night? He pictured the round black sphere in the moonlight on the kitchen table. Quickly clearing a spot on the shelf nearest to the light, Jevic set the rock gently upon it.

"Is that better?" he asked.

Instantly, the shimmer of an eye appeared on the rough surface, and Jevic coaxed, "It's okay, we're alone!"

The eye closed as the head slowly lifted, leaving a void in the round, dark surface. It turned to one side and then the other as though it was stretching. Then the left arm revealed itself, starting at the fingertips and working its way up past the elbow to the shoulder. Next, the right arm broke away, and with the flick of a tiny wrist, a golden blade emerged with an audible zing. Jevic flinched but held his ground as the rock completed its transformation into the perfectly marvelous little man he was waiting for.

Aaron, who appeared to be about thirty years of age, was dressed in a material that resembled black leather and shimmered with deep blue highlights. The tight-fitting armor-like suit had padding on the shoulders, chest, and elbows. For a little guy, he had an impressive air of confidence. Dark, shoulder-length hair hung cavalierly in front of his face, partially covering one eye. A hand clad in the same dark leather, but leaving the fingers exposed, brushed his locks aside. Undoubtedly, his sharp features added to his youthful appearance, but there was a deeper quality to this little man, an undeniable wisdom behind Aaron's dark eyes, that suggested he may be much older.

"That was awesome! How do you do that?" Jevic asked excitedly.

"I've never had to explain that to anyone before," Aaron answered hesitantly. "I'm not even sure I can. The ability to alter one's physical appearance is a gift that many from my realm possess. We are called Changers."

"Why didn't you change while I was holding you?"

"If a Changer transforms while in contact with a human, their gift could be stolen by the mortal." Aaron raised a brow. "That would be devastating to the Changer, and you can only imagine the mischief a human could manage with this ability."

"Do you always change into that rock?" Jevic asked.

"No. I can assume almost any form; mineral, plant, animal—even human. That's how we blend in. Most people never give a Changer a second glance."

"People see you like that," Jevic nodded at the little guy, "And they aren't curious?"

"Most are too preoccupied to notice anything around them, and it seems that the older they get the more likely they are to easily dismiss anything out of the ordinary as a figment of their imagination. Humans in general seem very preoccupied, disconnected, and reluctant to believe there's anything more to the universe than their own little piece of it."

"So why did you come back?" Jevic asked. "I'd nearly convinced myself you were something I only dreamed about."

Aaron glanced briefly at him. Then he began to pace slowly across the dusty shelf. "There was a time when only a thin veil of magic separated the earthly realms we live in. The nature spirits of my realm freely visited the human world, and occasionally, a clever human would cross into the spirit realm. There was a balance of awareness and respect between our worlds." Aaron paused, and there was sadness in his tone as he continued. "Until the day human greed breeched the veil; four sacred treasures were stolen from my people. The veil became impenetrable, and nearly all passage between our worlds ceased."

Bending one knee to the shelf, Aaron balanced his sword on point in front of him with his hands wrapped around the shimmering hilt. As he pulled it close to his chest, he locked eyes with the young man. "Ages passed," he continued, "Our realms, like two sides of the same coin, now know only stories of the other's existence. Yet to this day, half of the earth's spirits would destroy this world to punish mankind for stealing what was most sacred to them. However, the Seelies, my own people, believe there is hope for humanity, and if given a chance, they could use their abilities to benefit the earth."

Jevic interrupted, "What does this have to do with me?"

"Everything," Aaron replied. "For a thousand years, one prophecy and the promise it held for the future of our world has brought us hope. That prophecy speaks of one young human who will set things right."

Jevic shook his head, "Set things right? What does that mean?"

"The young man in that story is a Seer, like you," Aaron said as he rose to his feet. He turned on his heel and began to pace back and forth on the shelf once again. "You forced me to protect myself the other night," he said, holding the golden sword out into the light. "As I had hoped, this fulfilled the first part of that prophecy. Such a wound bestows the power of Sight. Only a few have ever received such a gift and all were destined to great purpose, as are you."

"What are you talking about? I'm only fifteen," Jevic argued.

Aaron laughed. "You underestimate yourself, my friend. Life is a grand journey that you've only just begun."

"Alicia tells me the same thing," Jevic commented, mostly to himself.

"Alicia, what a dear girl," Aaron said.

"She's ninety," Jevic informed.

"I remember when she first came to these woods," Aaron

LISA POPP

reminisced, seeming to completely ignore the young man's comment. "Her curls were the color of tiger lilies."

"How old are you?" Jevic asked.

"By your calendar, I'm 214 years," he replied.

"214!" Jevic echoed. "But you look so young."

"I am young, for my kind."

Not wanting to be rude, Jevic hesitated before asking, "Exactly what is your kind?"

"I'm Sidhe from a dimension of the Earth known as Fae, the Otherworld, or the spirit realm. Those who dwell there are more spirit than flesh. Because mankind's focus lies mainly on the physical plane, they tend to be somewhat oblivious to life forces like mine that share their world. Only Seers, like you and Alicia, are aware we exist."

"Wait! What? Alicia's a Seer?" Jevic interrupted, trying to make sense of what he'd heard. "She spoke to me about the faces in the trees, but she never mentioned them talking to her."

"You can hear the trees speak to you?" Aaron asked with great interest.

"Yes, but only when I touch them," Jevic answered.

"You were given two gifts," Aaron said excitedly. "How unusual! Very unusual...a Seer and a Keeper."

"What's a Keeper?"

Aaron stopped pacing long enough to slip his sword gracefully into its scabbard before he continued to stroll and explain, "Spirits of the earth, hidden from most mortal eyes, are visible to a Seer, but a Keeper is allowed to speak with them, learn from them. That is a very special honor, Jevic. The wisdom they share with you must be kept to yourself."

"I have to tell Alicia," he insisted.

"Tell no one else," Aaron warned.

Jevic nodded. Who else would he tell anyway? He couldn't think of a living soul who'd believe a story like this. In fact, he'd be crazy to breathe a word to anyone. He was quite overwhelmed, which was apparent in his expression. "Why me? I really don't understand any of this."

34

JEVIC AND THE STONE

"Follow your heart when your head is confused," Aaron advised. "Your path should begin with the Triad. It will be up to you to choose your steps from there. Meet me tomorrow morning beside the west brook, and I will take you there."

"Will you look like that or a rock or what?" Jevic asked.

"I'm not sure," Aaron replied with a wink. "Ask the trees where to find me." Then, with a brilliant flash of light he was gone.

"No!" Jevic shouted. As he grabbed a handful of air directly above the tiny footprints in the dust, a cricket hopped from the shelf onto the dirt floor and slipped beneath the door.

5 ~ DESTINY ~

That night, Jevic lay awake for hours, his mind jumbled with questions for which he had no answers. He finally abandoned his bed and sat alone in the living room waiting for morning to come. It was nearly seven o'clock. His grandmother was usually out of bed by then, so he knocked on her door. When there was no answer, he pushed it open and called her name softly as he entered the room.

White hair flowed over her pillow like drifts of snow, and there was an incredibly peaceful smile on the old woman's face. He whispered her name; a little louder a second time, but there was still no response. A wave of panic seized him. What if she's not just sleeping?

As he reached out to touch her shoulder, she faintly answered, "Yes, my dear," without opening her eyes.

He exhaled, "I was worried. You never sleep so late."

Alicia's green eyes opened slowly and a smile decorated her face. "Corbin, you should have woken me earlier."

Something inside of him squirmed. "Alicia, I'm Jevic," he whispered.

For a few seconds, she seemed to stare right through him, and then she shook her head. "Of course it's you, Jevic. I'm sorry, dear. I was dreaming so deeply I was confused for a moment," she admitted. "I'd better be getting up before somebody throws dirt in my face."

Jevic winced. He hated when she made jokes about dying, which she seemed to do more often lately.

"Feel like taking a walk?" he asked.

Alicia looked at the early morning sun streaming through the bedroom window. "Would you put the kettle on while I'll get dressed?" Her voice was weaker than usual. Was it because she had just woken up, or had she'd left a part of herself behind in that dream?

The kettle whistled, and Jevic filled Alicia's china teapot. The strings of two teabags steeping within dangled over hand painted clusters of wild flowers on the outside. He carefully set the lid into place and read the words written around the edge of it for at least the hundredth time. "All the flowers of all the tomorrows are in the seeds of today."

As he pondered the meaning of those words, Alicia shuffled stiffly into the kitchen and suggested they have their tea in the garden. That would be all she felt up to this morning. On days like this, he drank tea because it made her happy, not because he particularly enjoyed the taste. Besides, he was dying to talk to her about what had happened.

First, he carried the tea set out to the cast iron table in the center of the garden. Then Jevic helped Alicia, who leaned heavily on her cane as she made her way gingerly across the flagstone. Richly-colored moss grew between the flat gray stones, winding its way from one end to the other like strips of living carpet. When she was safely seated, he said, "I have something to tell you."

"Well, don't keep me wait'in," she replied.

Beginning with how he'd found the rock in the ferns, Jevic's story spilled out of him in an unstoppable stream of excitement. Finally taking a breath, he uttered, "They're amazing. Aren't they? You were right. I should have seen their faces before. They're so obvious that it makes me wonder what else I've been missing. I wish everyone could see things the way I can…the way we can," he corrected with a smirk.

No one else could have understood how he felt better than Alicia. She had kept her own story bottled up inside for decades, making it difficult for her to talk about at first. For the first time in all of those years, she had someone to tell how she'd pricked her finger on a tiny arrowhead hidden among Corbin's things after his death. Having been raised in Ireland, Alicia was familiar with the legends of elf-shot and had made the connection when she began seeing spirits soon after. Although she couldn't be sure, she may even have seen a little fellow fitting Aaron's description walking in the woods on more than one occasion.

"Where is that arrowhead now," Jevic asked.

"It's gone; disappeared from the box where Corbin had kept it. I never saw it before or again after that day," she told him while casually rubbing the tip of her finger.

"I don't understand why this is happening to me," Jevic admitted. "So, Aaron's taking me to meet the Triad later this morning." When those words left his lips, he noticed a change in Alicia's expression. There was an instant furrow in her brow and an unsettling, distant look in her eyes.

"Is there something wrong? Do you know what The Triad is?" he asked.

Alicia gently set down her cup and drew a shaky breath. "The Triad is a group of three trees; one oak, one ash and one hawthorn. Where these three grow together, you will surely find the good folk from the Otherworld," she informed him. "But I worry about you going there."

"Why?" he asked. "These are the woods I've spent my whole life in. I see things differently now, but that doesn't mean anything's changed."

A smile melted the furrow from the old woman's brow. "Yes, these woods are the same," she agreed. "The difference is that you've always stayed in the woods. Creatures like Aaron can travel beyond its borders to a world that you and I know nothing about. It could be very dangerous."

"I'm not afraid," he insisted. "If I can see this stuff, there must be a reason for it. I'd like to find out what that reason is."

"I've heard stories about people who visited the fairy realm, Jev. It's nothing like it is here. A person must know how to mind their manners not to offend the 'good folk.' For if they take offense in what you do or say, they can be nasty little boogers," she warned. "You should never eat or drink anything offered to you by these people, and be weary about trusting any of them because some are not at all fond of humans."

"They haven't met me yet," Jevic said with a smirk.

His grandmother's stern look suggested he heed her warning.

"Don't worry. I will be careful. I'll use my head. Is there anything else?" he asked.

Alicia hesitated before she answered, "Corbin was there before." Jevic's eyes widened and she continued to speak. "We'd been married for five years and were worried we might never have a family. Then one morn'in, Corbin heard someone calling his name. He followed that voice into the woods and didn't come home until after dark. By then I was frightened half to death. He'd met a little person near a hawthorn tree who had predicted we'd have a son within a year's time." Her eyes glazed over, and she reached into her sleeve for a hanky. "He also said that our son's son would have a single son upon whose shoulders the future of the world would one day come to rest."

"What?" Jevic choked. "You knew about this! Why didn't you tell me?"

"I couldn't say anything until I knew for sure that it was true," she justified. "A month later, I learned I was expecting, and Corbin began acting strangely, like he needed to protect us from something. He wouldn't talk about it. It was as though he knew exactly what the future had in store, but there was nothing he could do to change it. So he did his best to prepare for the inevitable. That's when he carved the doors for this garden."

The garden behind their old stone house was enclosed by a wall draped in vines and wild moss that had crept in from the woods. On opposing ends of this garden, stood two arched doorways, one lead into the kitchen and the other lead out to the woods. The wooden doors inside of these arches had hammered iron hinges and latches whose glossy black paint had been blemished by time. Centered in near the top of each was a small, amber-colored window divided into quarters by a Celtic cross. Beyond these similarities the doors were very different, each intricately carved with its own unique design.

The door to the cottage was covered with four-leaf clover. This one had always been of particular interest to Jevic because he had an uncanny knack for finding these four-leafed treasures growing wherever he went. They were supposed to bring good luck to those fortunate enough to find them, but not in Jevic's case. In fact, he'd come to believe they had the exact opposite effect for him. He didn't stop picking them but had learned to quickly pass the four leaves on to someone else before things started to go horribly wrong.

The image of an oak tree had been flawlessly hewn on the door that opened to the woods. Its branches were laden with clusters of scalloped leaves and acorns. Jevic still remembered the day he discovered there was a face subtly carved on the trunk of that oak. From then on, that was all he could see whenever he looked at it. It looked like an old man with a long straight beard, deep eyes with thick drooping lids, and a long, crooked nose. With time, he realized those eyes had an eerie way of following him no matter where he'd stand in the garden. But that had never made him uneasy until now. Why did Corbin carve these things? Was he trying to leave his family a message?

"On the very same day he hung the second door," Alicia continued, "A terrible storm blew in. Lightning hit a tree by the barn and a burning branch fell onto the roof. Corbin climbed up in the pouring rain to get it before the shingles caught fire. And...that's when he fell." Alicia stared into thin air as if she could see it happening all over again.

"I've always been afraid to ask you how it happened," Jevic said softly.

"There was more to that prophecy than he would tell me,"

she murmured. "Whatever it was, Jev, it terribly frightened him."

Jevic sat back into his chair. "Do you think he knew he was going to die?" he asked.

"I believe so," she answered vacantly.

"But he climbed onto that roof anyway?"

"Yes," Alicia acknowledged, wiping another tear with the hanky.

"Because there's no hiding from your own destiny, Alicia," he concluded. "Don't worry about me. This is just something I have to do," he said with an awkward smile.

Alicia rose from her seat and walked over to the flower bed where she pulled something from among the new sprouts growing there.

"Then take this with you," she told him, holding a perfect four-leaf clover out in the boy's direction. "You didn't find this one; it is a gift."

He popped out of his chair and took it from her. She could be right, he thought. This one may actually be lucky for me, but he would have kept it anyway.

Jevic pulled his hiking cap from his back pocket. The thing was a tattered old mess and starting to fit just a little too tight, but he seldom went anywhere without it. His dad had bought it for him when they went on their first hike together. There was a tear in the fabric on the front edge of the brim, creating a small pocket, into which he carefully slipped the stem of leaves. After giving her a peck on the cheek, he slapped the cap on his head.

"Who'll be crazy enough to mess with me now, huh?" he asked. Then he lifted his yet untouched cup of tea with his pinky extended, chugged it down in three huge gulps, and set it back down on the saucer.

Alicia smiled and started to caution him again, but he interrupted.

"I promise, I'll be back in time for lunch," he assured her.

After a long look at the face on the door between him and the woods, he pulled it open. Deep inside he still had doubts

41

that any of this was real. In fact, he'd half expected all the tree faces to be gone when he walked through that gate, or maybe he'd finally wake up. Either way he would have been wrong.

What he saw when he stepped out of the garden and into the woods was simply amazing. The spirit faces of the trees were everywhere he looked. All of his life, he'd felt surrounded by friends in these woods. Now he could actually see them. It was overwhelming and honestly somewhat uncomfortable. Should he speak to each one? It would be rude to just walk by like they were strangers in a crowd? After all, these were not strangers. For years he'd run past them, climbed through their branches, and sat in their shade. Had they always smiled so warmly at him?

A gentle breeze swept past, and a low branch from the young maple to his right brushed across Jevic's shoulder. Like the others, the face of that tree was looking directly at him.

"Hi," Jevic greeted. "Nice morning, isn't it?"

Grateful for the attention, the tree immediately appeared to respond.

"Wait!" Jevic told him as he pressed his palm against the gray bark.

"My name is Devin. It's good to see you again, Jevic," said the maple.

He answered, "Good to see you too, Devin."

As he walked away, he shook his head in disbelief. How could he not have seen them before? He wanted to meet them all, learn their names, and make the most of his new ability, but Aaron would be waiting for him. So he moved on, smiling and nodding at each tree he passed. At the slope leading down to the brook, he stopped. Looking upstream to the left and then down to the right, Jevic wondered where the wood elf might be waiting. An old hickory, whose face was barely visible among the shaggy strips of bark on his trunk, looked on from beside the well-beaten path. Jevic pressed his fingers against the scruffy looking tree. "Good morning! Do you know Aaron?" he asked.

"Yes. He told us you'd be looking for him," a gravelly voice responded. "He'll be by the flat rock falls."

Jevic knew exactly where that was and headed down the bank to his left. Sunshine danced on the brook water as it rolled slowly through this widest part of the valley. Mounded tufts of grass became stepping stones across the swampy ground. And as he passed the dogwood tree, his thoughts drifted back to Corbin, the great-grandfather he'd never known. Might he have known what would happen three generations in the future? Who had shared with him that prediction? How had they met? Did he also find a curious-looking rock in these woods?

The brook narrowed, and the ground around it was much drier. Jevic looked along the bank and up into the woods as he approached the flat rock falls, but there was no sign of Aaron. So he picked up a stick and began clearing clumps of dead leaves out of the brook. The water ran a bit faster each time he flipped a glob of debris from its path. As he jabbed it into another sloppy pile, a bright green frog hopped out into a small pool at the base of the falls. He watched curiously as the frog hopped several more times to reach the top of the terraced rocks.

Was that a real frog or was it just the form the Changer had taken for this occasion? He was so distracted by the possibility that he never noticed the long, dark shadow moving across the ground beside him until it stretched to the far side of the brook. Jevic spun around holding the stick out in front of him, with one slimy black leaf dangling from the other end.

"Whoa! Hang on. It's just me," Aaron said with a ring of amusement in his voice.

The angle of the morning sun had stretched the little fellow's shadow to a deceiving length. Having expected to see someone much larger, the boy lowered his gaze to the elf standing there.

Jevic was somewhat embarrassed and dropped the stick into the water. Then nodding in the frog's direction, he added, "I thought that might have been you."

Aaron raised a brow. "I don't do frogs," he informed him.

"Too many of them end up in some young boy's pocket."

"And rocks don't?" Jevic promptly asked.

The tiny man, impressed by the boy's quick wit, smiled broadly as he asked, "Are you ready? The Triad is anxious to meet you."

"As ready as I'll ever be," Jevic admitted.

"This way," Aaron said turning on his heel.

As the strange pair walked side by side toward the deepest part of the woods, Aaron cautioned Jevic to demonstrate the utmost respect to The Fairy-tree Triad. This was a part of the forest that Jevic rarely visited. It was over one too many hills, way too far for Alicia to walk, and out of ear shot if his mother were calling. Strangely, this was also the only part of the woods where his cell phone didn't work. And honestly, he'd never found anything interesting enough to lure him back there.

As they traveled beyond Jevic's comfort zone, he wondered what was waiting for him. Alicia had told him stories about fairies in Ireland. He'd read tales by the Brother's Grimm, poems by Robert Lewis Stevenson. Even William Shakespeare had written of the elemental spirits.

At the crest of a hill, Jevic heard what he thought were delicate wind chimes. But as he looked over the downward slope ahead of them, he realized nothing may ever again be what he expected. Three vaguely familiar trees grouped together on the hillside were shrouded in a mysterious glow. A ring of white birches stood in a near perfect circle around the three trees. Toad stools grew like spiral steps from the ground up into the branches of the birches, and seated on each of these fungal steps was at least one tiny person. Although differing in both size and appearance, the amazing creatures all radiated the same hypnotic glow in subtle, varying shades of color. It soon became obvious that the ringing, or singing, was also coming from these little beings.

"Unbelievable!" Jevic uttered. "It's more beautiful than anything I've ever seen," he whispered, as if what he was witnessing may all disappear if his presence were known.

"This is nothing," Aaron told him. "Follow me."

Jevic shadowed his little companion timidly into the center of the three trees, and the singing stopped. The oak was by far the largest tree he'd ever seen in these woods, and it took his breath right away when he recognized the spirit face upon it as the one from the garden gate. Forgetting all about minding his manners, the young man did not realize that he was staring slack jawed at the tree when Aaron kicked him in the ankle.

"Kneel down," the elf directed as he bent his own right knee to the ground.

Jevic snapped out of his trance and mimicked him.

"Head down, until they address you," Aaron instructed.

Jevic lowered his head slowly, giving the oak one last glance before his eyes met the ground in front of him.

A moment later, Aaron rose to his feet and said, "With me is Jevic O'Connor, who humbly seeks your guidance."

When he heard his name, Jevic kept his head low but lifted his eyes to peak between his long curls at the face of the great oak. He could see its lips moving but heard nothing at all.

"They've asked you to rise," Aaron told him.

Jevic's heart was pounding so hard he could see it through his shirt as he slowly rose to his feet and looked meekly at the oak. Its old eyes scanned the boy from head to toe and back again as if sizing him up. A creaking sound alerted him to movement overhead as one of the tree's lower limbs moved stiffly in his direction. When it stopped, a cluster of leaves hung right in front of him.

"Take one," Aaron instructed. "Take a leaf."

"No," Jevic argued. "How is that being respectful?" he asked. "That's like snatching a strand of hair from someone's head."

"You must," the elf insisted.

So with a deep breath, he reluctantly reached his left hand up and touched one of the leaves. As he did, he heard the oak's voice boom, "It is a great pleasure to finally meet you, Jevic O'Connor. My name is Osred. I am the divine advisor of the forest. Take the leaf you touch so that you may hear me speak to you."

Jevic gave the leaf a gentle tug and it snapped free from the branch. As the limb of the oak withdrew, he noticed movement in the ash tree to the right. Soon there was another branch before him with eight leaves aligned in pairs and a ninth centered alone at the very end. Without hesitating, he plucked the single leaf from the tip.

"I am very pleased to meet you, Jevic. My name is Oswin, meaning divine friend," said a gentle, feminine voice that perfectly suited the beautiful face on the ash. "Knowing who your true friends are will get you through the challenges you will face."

There was a rustling behind him before the ash had even withdrawn her branch, and Jevic peered over his shoulder for his first good look at the thorn tree. The hawthorn branch before him was covered in tiny, white blossoms. Among the uniquely fragrant flowers and saw-tooth leaves were needle-like thorns, and this time, he reached very carefully for the leaf he would take.

"I am Osmund, the divine protector," said the powerful voice of the hawthorn. "Jevic, the cane your great-grandmother carries was made from one of my branches. I will protect you as I have protected her. The staff that rests at my side is my gift to you, young warrior."

Jevic's mind raced as his gaze drifted from the spirit face to the wooden staff leaning against the thorn's trunk. Alicia's cane, the one that never left her side, had been a gift from this tree? He'd never asked where she'd gotten it; there was no reason to ask. It was as much a part of who she was as her snowy hair and emerald eyes. In fact, her cane was the one thing beside Corbin's pipe that she'd never part with. As the boy's thoughts churned, his feet brought him eye to eye with Osmund, who nodded reassuringly as the boy accepted his gift.

"Thank you," he whispered to the thorn as he bowed humbly at the waist.

Returning to his place beside Aaron, Jevic held the staff in his left hand at about shoulder height and rested the other end to the ground. Immediately, his fingers began to tingle and the wood became like clay in his fist. It was a terribly odd sensation, but no matter how he tried, his fingers would not open until the staff had molded to fit his hand perfectly. And then the wood hardened. The whole process took only seconds, and afterward, he could wiggle his fingers freely.

Jevic nodded to acknowledge the hawthorn's generous gift and that promise to protect him. Holding the three leaves in his right hand and the hawthorn staff, a little tighter, in his left, he heard Osred address him again.

"We have waited long for this day," the oak boomed.

"Why...Sir?" Jevic interrupted. "I don't understand any of this."

"Because there are wrongs that must be undone, with your help," Osred replied.

Feeling rather inadequate, Jevic asked, "How can I help?"

"Hundreds of years ago, four treasures were stolen from the Sidhe, the elemental spirits of this earth. These were sacred to the Sidhe and each possesses an extraordinary power. The Stone of Destiny, one of those treasures, must be returned before the spirit realm is seized by darkness," the oak answered. "We know nothing of its whereabouts, except that it's in the mortal realm. Since it was first taken, the Sidhe have had hope in a prophecy that says you will return what is sacred to them."

"Me? Why do they think it's me?" Jevic asked.

"You bear the name of the victorious young warrior of legend, and you are blessed with the gifts of Seer and Keeper. All of this has been foretold."

"If nobody's seen these things for hundreds of years, how am I supposed to find them?" he asked.

Oswin answered, "First, you must learn who your friends are, for they will protect you from your enemies."

"And you must learn to protect yourself in a world that will show you no mercy," the hawthorn warned. "The dark spirits will stop at nothing to see you fail. They plan to destroy the world, and only you can stop them."

"What?" Jevic snapped at the hawthorn, forgetting proper

conduct altogether.

"It is true, Jevic," Osred confirmed. "If the dark spirits have their way, all life on earth will be destroyed to eradicate mankind."

"This sounds like something the grown-ups should handle," Jevic argued. "Maybe the FBI or the United Nations or…"

"Of all earth's creatures, mankind poses the greatest threat and yet promises the greatest hope. Adults of your species can lose track of what truly matters. And often, the more there are of them the more useless they become," Osred suggested. "The prophecy reads, 'One young man will return The Stone.' Sometimes, Jevic, less is more."

"The realms of the earth are bound to one another," Oswin added. "The mortal realm cannot exist without elemental spirits to nurture life on the surface. The unholy, Unseelie, spirits will let everything die if they take the throne. Only the sacred Stone can prevent that from happening."

Jevic suddenly felt like there was an elephant sitting on his chest. He struggled to breathe and frantically raked his fingers through his hair. "Isn't this a lot to expect from one guy my age?" he asked, without directing the question to anyone in particular.

But it was the little man at his side who simply answered, "Yes."

Jevic's palms began to sweat, like they do when he has to talk to a pretty girl or give a presentation in front of the class. How he wished that was all that was expected of him now. The trees waited silently for his response. The tiny creatures in their branches also waited.

"Where would I begin?" Jevic asked.

"With a promise," the great oak replied. "The Stone of Destiny must be returned, and you must promise to do everything in your power to retrieve it. Are you willing to make such a promise?"

He looked at the faces of the Triad and then down at Aaron. His eyes blurred as they swept through the forest filled with life.

"Of course, I promise," Jevic replied. "I'll help you find The Stone."

Osred's face glowed, for it seemed that the prophecy was indeed being fulfilled. "Then let your quest begin," he proclaimed.

With his words, the audience seated in the trees erupted with fairy song. The air became charged with such energy that the hair stood up on the back of the young human's neck, and then the ground beneath his feet began to tremble.

"What's happening?" he asked Aaron.

"They're opening the hill for you. It's a gateway to the Otherworld," the elf replied.

Jevic looked desperately from side to side and tightened his grip on the hawthorn staff as the forest floor around the oak quaked. Oswin's friendly smile briefly caught his eye. But he was awestruck as the oak giant rose several feet up out of the ground, revealing both an opening beneath its roots and a brilliant light from within.

A multitude of fairies poured from the trees in a kaleidoscope of color, and then they were gone.

What just happened? Is any of this real, Jevic asked himself? His head was still reeling with questions, amazement and fear. And then he remembered the promise he'd made to Alicia. But wasn't the promise he'd just made to The Triad more important? She'd understand, he hoped.

Jevic drew a ragged breath and looked down at the little elf at his side. "I guess we can't keep destiny waiting," he said, "Can we?"

Aaron shook his head and walked toward the gateway beneath the oak.

"Yeah, I didn't think so," Jevic mumbled. He tightened his grip on his hawthorn staff and took his first step toward the unknown.

Osmund the hawthorn raised a brow and rolled his gaze slowly from the ash to the oak. "The kid's a little shaky. Do you really believe he's the one?"

Osred's eyes shimmered with hope. "It does not matter what anyone else believes. It's up to him now."

6 ~ THE OTHERS ~

Jevic's knees were shaking so badly that he was already thankful for the wooden staff. He took one last look at the forest behind him, tucked the three leaves safely inside of his pocket, and stepped through the opening beneath Osred's roots.

The entrance was framed in white marble with beautifully detailed carvings that Jevic was too terrified to appreciate. In fact, if he stopped to think about anything, even for a second, he knew he'd probably change his mind about this altogether and turn around while he still had a chance. A few unusual winged creatures, extraordinary knotted borders and flowery vines were all he could make out at a glance.

So intense was the light within the hill that it took several seconds for his eyes to adjust. As they did, he could see that the corridor he'd entered was about eight feet wide with a strong downward pitch. The floor was not dirt, as he would have expected to find beneath the roots of the oak. It was flat mortared stone, polished to an impressive shine that reflected the brilliant light pouring out of the walls around him. The most glorious music echoed up out of the corridor, although he recognized neither the words nor the melody.

"How long is this passageway?" Jevic asked, turning to look

down at Aaron. However, instead of the tiny man who'd followed him into the passageway, there stood a human-sized pair of boots, legs, a torso and a head that looked exactly like him. Understandably, Jevic was petrified. He stood staring at the man dressed head to toe in leathery armor with a familiar gold sword sheathed at his side and couldn't move a muscle.

Entertained by the look of utter dismay on Jevic's face, Aaron struggled to contain his laughter. "It is I," he managed to convey before a chuckle escaped him.

"Another disguise?" the boy asked.

"No. This is what I really look like," Aaron replied, struggling to control his amusement. "I prefer being myself, especially when I'm home."

"Thanks for warning me!" Jevic snapped. "What the hell? Don't you think I've got enough to deal with here?" he scolded Aaron, who was now six feet tall.

"You're right. I should have warned you," Aaron agreed with a relentless smirk.

"At least you'll be easier to keep track of now, I was afraid of stepping on you before," Jevic mumbled. After the initial shock, he could appreciate the humor in the situation and shook his head with a laugh before extending his right hand. "It's nice to meet you, Aaron," he said, "That is your name, isn't it?"

Aaron's glove clapped against the boy's hand and his fingers tightened powerfully around it. "It is my name, and it is my pleasure," he told him.

The Changer seemed to radiate an energy the boy had never before witnessed in another living creature. Maybe it was because of everything that was happening. Maybe he was just freaked out by the size of this guy now. But as they shook hands, Jevic felt a charge ripple through him that made his hair stand on end. His heart seemed determined to beat its way through his ribs, and he wondered if Aaron could hear it echoing off of the wall beside them.

"We'd best keep moving. They expect us down there," Aaron added with a nod.

Jevic, still so amazed by the Changer's new appearance, had to make a comment. "You sure don't look 214 years old. You eat a lot of vegetables or what?"

"Time is different here," Aaron explained as they walked. "We live at least a thousand years."

"A thousand years!" Jevic gasped. "Are you married? Do you have a family?"

"I'm not married, and you'll soon meet my parents," Aaron answered.

As the music grew louder, Jevic began to smell flowers, vibernum and lilacs. These same plants were blooming in his family's garden, but they were underground. He was beginning to wonder exactly what he was walking into when the corridor took a sharp turn to the right and opened abruptly into the Otherworld.

It wasn't a room as he'd expected but an entire countryside that stretched out in front of them. Lush vegetation grew everywhere, not only up from the ground but down from the glowing dome overhead as well. Behind this sky-like dome were the shadowy roots from the forest above. Where they sprouted through the ethereal veil-like sky, leaves and flowers grew just as they did from branches on the surface; although these colors were incredibly more vibrant.

Directly in front of them was a courtyard with a beautiful mosaic floor the size of a soccer field. Bordered with a Celtic knot design of blues and greens, the image featured at the center was one Jevic recognized as the Tree of Life. A symbol of oneness with all things in nature, the tree is bound to the Earth yet forever reaches toward the heavens.

The branches and roots were braided into a ring that encircled the entire tree—each branch in the circle eventually becoming a root and each root becoming a branch. It was a beautifully simple interpretation of how we are all connected. And obviously, this tree held great meaning to these people, for the symbol in the center of the courtyard was nearly forty feet in diameter and shimmered as if made of pure gold.

As Aaron walked toward the center of the courtyard, the

hundreds of Sidhe who had been dancing and singing fell silent. The crowd parted down the middle to let them pass, and the young human tried his best not to make direct contact with the ocean of eyeballs that were locked on him.

"Why is it so quiet all of the sudden?" he asked.

"They are curious about you, Young Warrior," Aaron told him.

Jevic realized he was very curious himself. What did elementals look like anyway? He glanced quickly at a few of the faces on the edge of the crowd. Many looked like regular people but varied greatly in size from a few inches to six or seven feet tall. Others appeared to be dressed in odd costumes, or perhaps the oddities were their own. Either way, several possessed physical characteristics of plants or animals. One boyish face wore a black mask over his eyes as he fiddled nervously with the raccoon tail growing from his back side. A group of slender green-skinned people had large flower blossoms sprouting from the tops of their head while a much shorter girl's head was covered with a wild brown tangle of hair mixed with oak leaves. And as unusual as these creatures appeared, every face reflected the same warm, ever-present glow of this place.

Jevic's thoughts were out-racing his heart now. This was either the experience of a lifetime or he was losing his mind. Aaron's words, "Young Warrior," suddenly bothered him and the he felt he needed to be honest.

"Yeah, about that," Jevic said uncomfortably. "I'm really not much of a fighter. Are you sure it's me that you've been expecting?"

"Hah. The strength of a warrior is in here," Aaron told him, slapping Jevic on the chest, "And in here," he added, rubbing a gloved hand over the curls on top of the young man's head. "Trust me, you're the one."

As they walked together up the trunk of the tree sparkling brightly beneath their feet, Jevic had to ask, "Is that real gold?"

"Yes," Aaron replied matter-of-factly, without as much as a change of expression.

"Oh," Jevic said, feeling, if possible, even more uncomfortable. Suddenly, his mouth felt a little dry. He stepped gingerly on his way across the golden tiles while keeping pace with his companion who was the only, although vaguely, familiar thing he had to hang on to in this place.

On the far end of the courtyard was a wide set of stairs leading up to what Jevic presumed to be a palace; an assumption based solely on images he'd seen in movies and video games; for the world he was from had nothing that could compare to the structure before him. In front of the palace, two thrones were centered on an elevated marble landing. Upon the left throne was seated an extremely handsome old gentleman wearing sparkling white robes trimmed in gold and green. He wore a large golden crown on top of his head, and Jevic was suddenly quite aware of his own casual attire.

The throne on the right held an angelic looking woman, probably close to the king's age, but so incredibly gorgeous that she took the boy's breath away. She was dressed in a gossamer blue gown, more beautiful than any dress Jevic had ever seen. Her hair was like spun silver, wrapped tightly into a tall bun on top of her head, which was encircled by a crown of clear uncut crystals that danced with rainbows as she turned to smile warmly at the young visitor.

Jevic's palms were sweaty and his knees wobbly again as he followed Aaron up the steps. When they reached the top, he watched Aaron drop down onto his right knee before the thrones and followed suit; mindful to keep his head down until they addressed him.

"Your Highness, may I introduce our guest to you?" Aaron asked.

"Please do," the king replied; his voice was weak but enthusiastic.

"Jevic," Aaron called, and the boy raised his eyes cautiously. "I'd like you to meet my parents."

Jevic's head whipped up to focus on Aaron, who gave him a wink. He couldn't believe what was happening. A few days ago he was enjoying the sun on his face at Apple Rock, minding his own business. All he did was pick up a rock—a rock, an elf, a cricket, a muscle-bound warrior. And now, on top of all that, this guy was a prince? He didn't know whether to chew him out for keeping this little secret too or ask for his autograph.

As Jevic stood up to approach the thrones, he leaned toward Aaron and whispered through clenched teeth, "You're just full of surprises."

"King Ronan, Queen Nia, this is Jevic O'Connor," Aaron formally introduced. "Jevic O'Connor, this is my father, King Ronan and my mother, Queen Nia."

"Welcome, Jevic," the king greeted warmly. "We are honored that you have agreed to help us." He spoke softly, but Jevic had a feeling he was by no means a man to be taken lightly.

"Thank you, your Highness," he replied. "I hope I'm able to help."

"I'm sure you have many questions," said the old king. "Let's walk through the garden where it's more private."

"Thank you, Sire," Jevic answered. He was uncomfortable enough just being there, but speaking with a king was more than he'd expected, and he greatly appreciated being able to do it without a crowd watching his every move.

The royal family walked their special guest through the gated entrance of an enclosed palace garden. The familiar sense of security Jevic associated with his own family's garden washed over him with a welcome, calming effect. For the first time since he'd been introduced to the Triad, his knees didn't feel like they were made of Jell-O. Although in the company of three individuals who were very different from anyone he'd ever known, he was surprisingly comfortable.

King Ronan seemed grateful for the boy's presence, maybe even hopeful. But there was something else behind the king's reassuring smile that Jevic couldn't quite interpret.

"Let me first explain where you are," King Ronan said. "This place has been known by many names: Fae, the Fairy

Realm, the Otherworld, and the Spirit Realm are just a few." He tapped a golden Tree of Life, which hung from a chain in the center of his chest. "Like the roots of the great tree, we dwell below the surface and support all life above. Nothing lives without the spirit of the Earth flowing through it. Do you understand?" he asked.

"Yes, Sir," Jevic replied.

The king continued, "Where the veil between our worlds is thin, those above enjoy occasional glimpses into the spirit realm. Spirit is a word humans use, but few truly understand. Over the past several hundred years, man's knowledge of our realm has been reduced to myths and children's stories; neither is taken seriously." The king walked over to a bench and carefully sat. "My people are the Sidhe," he continued, "Like you; we are spirits of this Earth, but without your physical limitations. This is how Aaron is able to manipulate his appearance; not by changing his physical presence but by changing the way you view his energy," he paused briefly to assess the boy's comprehension. Jevic nodded, and the king continued.

"The more the world above advances its knowledge of the physical, the more detached it becomes from Spirit. Humans have forgotten that they are just a part of the universe, not the center of it." King Ronan's tone was stern and he pointed again to the tree medallion. "Human arrogance and greed reached a dangerous point when the four sacred treasures of my people were stolen. Since then, our world has been divided."

The king slowly left the bench and began to pace back and forth on the path in front of it. "Many believe old age does not come to those who dwell here." He turned to look directly at Jevic. "It comes," he said softly. "But age is a friend that brings with it experience and wisdom. We all move along the path life puts before us. Soon, my path will take me to the branches that reach into the heavens." He glanced briefly toward the dome overhead. "I do not know who took these treasures, but it is time they were returned. These treasures are sacred to us, Jevic;

possessing powers we have greatly missed for a thousand years: the Stone of Destiny, the Sword of Light, the Spear of Lugh, and Dagda's Cauldron. One in particular must be returned quickly."

"The Stone of Destiny," Jevic concluded. Worried he had spoken out of turn, he looked at Aaron, who smiled approvingly.

"Yes," the king said. "You see, the Stone will let the world know who the next ruler of this realm is to be. He need only rest so much as a finger upon it. Without the Stone, my kingdom will collapse after my passing. Our enemies will take advantage of my empty throne, and there will be war. My people cannot defend themselves without a leader."

Jevic was confused. "Why won't Aaron take the throne?" he asked.

"I pray that will happen," the king answered, "But without the Stone's approval, it is forbidden."

"I don't know where to begin," Jevic admitted.

King Ronan closed his eyes and outstretched his hands palm up in front of the young man. Jevic watched in utter amazement as an image of the Stone of Destiny appeared in the air above them. It was a rectangular block of white marble, about the size of a small footstool. Jevic tried to memorize every detail. He walked closer and could see the Tree of Life carved into the top of it. There was also script, characters he did not recognize, sandwiched between two horizontal bands of a beautifully knotted design. The image was so realistic that Jevic reached out to touch it. When he did, it vanished.

The king opened his eyes and folded his hands in front of him. "Remember, the Stone is powerful," he said, "It will make itself known to the one who wants to bring it home. But I caution you; there are those from the dark side of this realm who will be looking for it too. The sacred Stone is all that stands between them and my throne."

Jevic didn't know exactly how to ask, but he needed to know how much time he had. As he struggled with the words, King Ronan began to smile knowingly.

"You don't have very long, Jevic. I fear this will be my last summer," the king told him.

Can he read my thoughts, Jevic wondered? Why not? He just projected that image of the Stone in thin air.

Suddenly, the wonderful smell of fresh baked bread seized Jevic's attention. A young woman, carrying a silver tray, had appeared without notice and was talking with the queen.

"That will be fine, thank you," Queen Nia said, as the woman set the tray down on the bench. "Jevic, would you like some fresh bread and jam?" the queen offered politely.

He remembered Alicia's warning, but the bread smelled delicious. With all that had happened that morning, he'd forgotten to have breakfast. If the Sidhe trusted him to find their missing treasure, why would they poison him? Besides, it would be terribly rude to refuse the queen's offer.

"Yes, please," he answered.

She encouraged him to help himself, but the breads and assorted spreads on the tray all looked scrumptious. The tray gleamed brightly, and the knife beside each silver cup of jam looked like it had never been used. Jevic hesitated, trying to imagine the proper manners one should use when eating in front of royalty.

Aaron stepped up beside him and said, "Great, I'm starving. Jevic, try the apple butter, it's my favorite."

The teenager watched as the prince smeared a large slice of warm bread with golden apple butter, cut it in half and handed one to him.

"Thanks!" Jevic said.

The bread was still warm and as light as a feather. He heard Alicia's warning once more, just before he bit into it. The boy's mouth had never known such sheer delight. There were no words to describe such absolute perfection in flavor. It was so incredible that it was gone before he realized he'd taken more than that first bite.

"I told you it was good," Aaron chuckled. "Have another."

Jevic didn't care about proper etiquette any more. He grabbed another slice, slapped a big glob of spread on it and enjoyed every bite. After his third, he wondered if people choose to stay here on their own accord once they'd tasted the food in this place.

"Would you like something to drink?" Queen Nia sweetly asked.

"No thank you, ma'am, I mean, your Majesty. The bread was delicious!" Jevic told her, "I think I'd better be going home now." He looked for Aaron's reaction.

"Wait," King Ronan commanded, "You can't go yet."

A tidal wave of panic swept through the boy. Perhaps they didn't plan to let him leave at all. Alicia had told him stories about people who were kept captive after stepping into a fairy ring or eating their food.

"Before you go, I have something for you, Jevic," the king said. He pulled an ornate pouch from his pocket and handed it to his guest.

It felt like silk and had beautiful leaves stitched in gold and silver thread on the fabric. As he admired it, he recognized the shapes were of oak, ash and hawthorn leaves like the ones he'd forgotten about in his pocket.

"Open it," Ronan directed.

Having been so intrigued with the packaging, Jevic hadn't considered what was inside. He loosened the drawstring and emptied the contents, a pile of gold chain, into his hand. Pinching the chain carefully between his thumb and forefinger, he lifted it slowly into the air. Swinging gracefully at the bottom was a golden medallion, exactly like the one the king wore around his neck. The boy looked over at Aaron and then toward King Ronan.

"I don't know what to say," Jevic stammered, not wanting to in anyway offend these people. "But I don't think I can accept such a gift."

"It is a token of our thanks to you, and you cannot return what is already yours. Look at the back," Ronan suggested.

Jevic flipped the medallion over. Carved into the gold were the words, "Jevic, Victorious Young Warrior." He couldn't believe it. Jevic slipped the chain over his head, saying humbly,

"Thank you, Sire."

"That medallion will be recognized by my people in this realm as well as in your own. With it, you may enter the doorway beneath the oak whenever you wish. Do not let it out of your hands for it holds power my enemies greatly desire," the king warned.

"I won't let it out of my sight," Jevic promised.

As he looked at the medallion lying against his chest, it somehow made everything else seem real. Maybe this wasn't a dream. Could he possibly be the guy the Seelies thought he was?

"My name was already on the back," Jevic said. "How did you know I would come?"

The king smiled. "That name has been there for over a thousand years," he replied. "Jevic was also my brother's name. He was lost in the last great battle with the Unseelie tribes. Beware of them, Jevic. They too possess powers of this world. But unlike us, they despise humans. There is nothing more dangerous than an enemy who is blinded by hate, except one that has nothing to lose."

The king rested his hand on the boy's shoulder and gave it a squeeze. "If they should recover the Stone before you, this world will fade into darkness under their rule. Aaron cannot always be with you. So you must be careful who you trust," he warned.

Jevic nodded quietly, but his mind was racing. The king's brother had his name. That is only a name. Were they sure he was the Jevic they were waiting for? There must have been others in a thousand years, or were there? Either way, these spirits believed he would help them. He had to believe it too; he'd given his word.

"Thank you, your Highness. I will…"

"I know you will, Jevic," the king interrupted. With those words, he turned and walked slowly toward the palace.

"It was very nice meeting you, Jevic," said Queen Nia, touching his arm lightly on her way to catch up with the king.

"It was nice to meet you too," he mumbled as if from a

daze.

As the palace doors swallowed the lovely old couple whole, Jevic panicked. God, is this really happening? What if I can't do what they expect of me? I can't breathe. I'm going to be sick, he thought.

Just then, Aaron put his hand on the boy's shoulder. "Are you all right?" he asked.

"I haven't completely lost my mind, have I?" Jevic whispered.

"You just need some time to sort everything out," Aaron told him. "Let's get you back home."

"That sounds like a great idea," Jevic agreed. The emotions he had welling up inside were overwhelming. As they walked back down the steps and across the courtyard, he wondered quietly. How would he ever be able to find their sacred Stone? Where would he even begin to look?

"Aaron," he asked, "How bad are the Unseelies your father mentioned?"

"You have good and evil in your world too. My people are the Seelies, meaning blessed, they look for the good in others and follow the light. The Unseelies, or unblessed, hate the good in others and prefer to dwell in the darkness," Aaron told him.

"Can they come into my world?" Jevic asked reluctantly.

"Yes," Aaron responded.

"Can they change into any shape like you can?"

"Some of them," the prince answered.

"Then how can I tell they're evil?" Jevic asked. There was a renewed sense of panic in his voice.

"That's where it gets tricky," Aaron said. "I suggest you use your heart when your head is confused. I've found that to be helpful. Evil cannot hide itself from you completely; you will feel it."

With one deep breath, the familiar smell of the woods began to settle Jevic's troubled mind. Somehow everything would work out. A single beam of sunshine cut its way through the cloudy sky and reflected off of his medallion. Jevic quickly slipped it under his shirt where it wouldn't be seen, and he could feel it against his skin. Then he pulled the silk pouch from one of his pockets and the three leaves of the triad from another. After carefully sliding the leaves into the pouch, he drew the string closed and tucked it away.

He turned to give the doorway beneath the oak one last glance, but Osred looked normal. Normal, he thought. Would anything ever again be normal? He paid his respects to the three great trees of the Triad and was on his way. With his staff in hand and his mind churning wildly, Jevic headed home, hoping he wasn't terribly late for lunch.

Alicia met him at the door with a hug. "Back so soon! Is everything all right?" she asked, taking a good look at him. "You are all right, aren't you?"

"I'm fine. I just have a lot to think about," he told her. "Sorry I'm late for lunch."

"Lunch, ya only left half an hour ago," Alicia told him.

Jevic was bewildered. "I've been gone for hours. I was sure it must be close to dinner time by now."

Half an hour was the time it would take to walk to the triad and back. He double checked the clock on the living room wall and tried to guess how long he'd been beneath the hill. It was 9:15. He checked another clock, just to be sure, but it read the same time as the first.

"Jev, what's the matter?" Alicia asked.

"I don't understand. I've been gone for hours, not minutes. Alicia, I've been gone for hours," he insisted.

Alicia took him by the hand and sat down beside him on the sofa. "I've heard stories about how time stops when you're there. You did go then?"

"Yes." Jevic looked around the room. "Where are Mom and Dad?"

"They dressed and went out for breakfast. I told'em I didn't want to go. Tell me. Tell me everything," she urged.

Jevic shook his head and blew a breath of air up into his bangs that sent his curls flying. "I don't know where to begin. The Triad is amazing! There were hundreds of fairies, little people, everywhere watching from the trees," he told her. Then he remembered what Aaron had said about repeating anything he'd been told by the spirits. It was difficult, but he only described where he went and what he saw. The stories King Ronan had shared with him about the Sidhe, and especially the fact that he'd eaten some of their food, he kept to himself.

"This was a gift from the hawthorn tree," he told her, holding up the wooden staff. He described the first time he held it and how it had formed to fit his hand perfectly.

Alicia gasped and put her hand over her mouth. "My cane did the same thing," she squealed. "I've never been able to tell a soul about that for fear they'd think I'd lost my senses."

Jevic smiled and told her, "I'd have believed you."

"Of course, you would have," she cried. "But what did they tell you about this purpose you have?" she asked.

Jevic didn't know what to say. He'd never lie to her, but he didn't want to worry her either. Besides, that was all part of those things he shouldn't repeat.

"The whole thing's kinda like a puzzle actually," he told her. "I'm not exactly sure how to explain it."

Alicia raised a wise, old brow. "I see," she said. "Ahh, you can't be talking about it?"

Jevic was ashamed for holding back.

"You do what you must, my dear. If they have a purpose for you, I'm sure it isn't to be blabbing everything to an old bat like me," she laughed. "I understand." Alicia reached out and gave his hand a squeeze. "I'll be here if you need me."

Jevic really wanted to cry. "I think I'll just go to Apple Rock to think for a while," he told her, and he did.

7 ~ GOOD INTENTIONS ~

The next morning, Jevic sat with his head against the window as the bus rolled to a stop at Brent's house. He rubbed his fingers over the medallion hidden under his shirt. It was going to be hard not telling him about everything that had happened.

"Morn'in Jev," Brent said, as he plunked down into the seat. "What's up?"

"Not much. The Johnson triplets have been messing with the bus driver again. We had to pull over once already," Jevic reported. "Those three sure are fearless."

"Robert Reilly's dad called my house while we were working on the cabin Saturday," Brent told him. "He told my dad that I assaulted his son in the cafeteria last week, threatened to press charges. I swore to my dad that I never laid a hand on the jerk. But I have a feeling I haven't heard the end of this yet."

"You've got to be kidding," Jevic said. "How does that guy get off being such an idiot his whole life and think he can turn the blame on everyone else?"

Jevic had a full schedule at school, so he planned to eat a quick lunch and sneak down to the computer lab to search for information on the Stone. He'd be the first to admit that it was a long shot. But the Internet was the best source of information he knew of, and he had no idea where else to start. He washed down his bologna sandwich with cold chocolate milk and told Brent he had to go use the lab for a project.

"I'll catch up with you later," Brent said.

Jevic brought his tray to the window and was halfway out the cafeteria door when he heard the commotion. Robert Reilly, backed up by a couple of his goons, Doug Smith and Phil Jackson, was standing nose to nose with Brent.

"Oh no," Jevic whispered, breaking into a full sprint back toward his table.

"You're nothing but a loser like the rest of your family," Reilly yelled.

"Reilly, you'd better watch your mouth before you end up on your back looking up at me again," Brent warned.

"Go ahead," Reilly yelled, "See where that will get you."

Brent smiled as he turned to walk away from the three trouble makers.

"Don't turn your back on me," Reilly shouted. There was a look of fury on his face that denied any chance that he'd be willing to let this blow over. "Let's see you smile with half your teeth knocked out," he threatened.

Brent turned back to face him and caught a sucker punch right in the eye. His head jerked sideways, but he came right back with a left hook to Reilly's jaw. Smith grabbed Brent from behind and Jackson's right fist was half way to Brent's face when Jevic hit Jackson like a freight train. Jackson sailed across the floor on his back, and Jevic scrambled to his feet like a cat. Smith had Brent's arms pinned behind him while Reilly was landing repeated body shots.

Jevic grabbed a tray from the table and whipped it, like a Frisbee, at Reilly. The tray hit him hard in the side. Brent tossed his head backwards into Smith's face. He immediately released Brent's arms and threw his hands over his nose.

Just then, Principal Lewis raced into the cafeteria. Within only seconds, the crowd that had formed around the fight scattered, and the five young men were on their way to the office to sort things out.

"I think O'Connor broke my ribs," Reilly shouted at the principal. "I want to press charges. I want to call my father," he demanded.

"I'd like to hear exactly what happened first," Principal Lewis told him. Just then the school nurse came into the office. She handed an ice pack to Smith for his nose, which was already twice its usual size.

"Get over here and check my ribs," Reilly barked.

The nurse asked, "Is that how you ask someone for their help?"

"I'm not asking you, I'm telling you," Reilly shouted.

"One more word out of you and you will be suspended, Mr. Reilly," Principal Lewis told him.

"My father is the President of the School Board," Reilly snapped, "I won't be suspended. It's more likely that you'll be looking for a new job, Lewis."

Principal Lewis's face was scarlet. He called his secretary over the intercom and asked her to get Mr. Reilly's father on the phone. The nurse lifted Reilly's shirt and barely touched his side.

"What are you trying to do, puncture my lung, you stupid hag?" he screamed.

Jevic looked at Brent sitting in the chair next to him. Under his left eye was all red and swollen. He took the second ice pack the nurse had brought with her from the desk in front of them and tossed it to Brent.

"Thanks," Brent replied, wincing as the cold touched his face.

The principal looked around the room at the five teens and shook his head. "We will contact all of your parents immediately to inform them of this incident. You five will meet me here first thing in the morning after everyone has had a chance to cool off and seek medical attention if necessary," he instructed through gritted teeth.

Reilly and Smith went to the nurse's office to wait for their parents to pick them up. The nurse had a chance to look at Brent's eye quickly before she left the room. He insisted he'd be all right and thanked her. The other three guys were told to return to class.

"How's your eye?" Jevic asked Brent as they walked down the hall.

"It's fine. My sisters hit harder than he does," Brent laughed. I should have known better than to turn my back on a jerk like that. Thanks for jumping in."

"Don't mention it," he said patting Brent on the shoulder.

By the next morning, the principal had several witnesses come forward to give their account of the incident in the cafeteria. Not surprisingly, Heather and Christina were the first ones to volunteer. To avoid further complications, the principal called Jevic and Brent into his office before the other three.

"Good morning, gentlemen," he said as they walked in and took a seat. He looked up from his desk and noticed the bruise under Brent's eye. "How are you feeling today, Mr. Thomas?"

"I'm fine," Brent replied.

"Good," Principal Lewis continued. "Then perhaps you could tell me how this all started."

"Reilly treats everybody like crap and gets away with it," Brent said. "When somebody tries to put him in his place, he doesn't like it very much."

"I see," the principal said with the slightest hint of a smile.

"And you, Mr. O'Connor," he asked, "You've never gotten yourself into any trouble like this before. What do you have to say?"

Jevic looked the principal right in the eye. "I've never had three creeps gang up on my friend either."

"Yes, I've heard what happened from several students. It does seem that Mr. Reilly and his buddies were looking for trouble," the principal acknowledged. "However, Mr. Smith has suffered a broken nose, and Mr. Reilly has sustained two cracked ribs."

Jevic and Brent looked away from the principal long enough to exchange a brief moment of satisfaction.

"I understand that this was self-defense on your part, but if there are any further problems with Mr. Reilly, come to me about it. We will do what we can to settle the dispute peacefully."

"Yes, Sir," they answered.

Brent stood up and held his hand out. "Thank you, Sir." Principal Lewis shook his hand and tried not to smile.

But the principal wasn't smiling at all when he shook Jevic's hand. "Reilly is not taking those cracked ribs lightly, Jevic. You keep a safe distance from that young man until things cool off."

"I will. Thank you, Sir."

When they walked into the hall, Jevic asked Brent, "You don't suppose those guys would take that broken nose and two cracked ribs as lesson learned, do you?"

"Probably not, but we might have them thinking twice before they try anything again," Brent laughed, nudging Jevic with his elbow.

"Yeah, got my dad thinking too," Jevic said.

"Is he mad?" Brent asked.

"I explained what happened, and it helped a little. But he sure didn't take that call from the school very well yesterday."

"Sorry, dude. Should I come by and talk to him?"

"No. I'll work it out, thanks."

Later in the cafeteria, Jevic sat at his usual table. He'd just started his lunch when someone pulled out the chair beside him and set down a tray. He expected it was Brent and didn't even look up from his meal, until he noticed the smell of perfume. When he did look up, there stood Heather smiling down at him.

"Mind if I sit here?" she asked.

"Uh, no. Go ahead," Jevic said, scanning the room uncomfortably for his buddy.

"I thought that maybe you could use some peace-loving company to keep you out of trouble while you eat today," she teased.

"That's probably not a bad idea," he agreed.

Heather sat quietly for only a few seconds before she turned to Jevic and asked, "Did you get into much trouble because of what happened?"

"No. Not here anyway. My dad wasn't too happy about the whole thing," he said. "I heard you talked to the principal. Thanks. I'm sure that helped."

"It was nothing," Heather said as she sliced the tomatoes in her salad into bite-sized pieces.

Just then the chair across the table from Jevic pulled out, and Brent set his tray down. "Hi, Jev. What's up?" he asked with a smirk from ear to ear.

Jevic grinned. "Not much. How about you?"

By the look on Brent's face, Jevic knew that he was not going to let the new addition to their lunch table go without some embarrassing remark, and braced himself for whatever Brent was going to throw at him. But then, Christina set her tray down on the table next to Brent's and pulled out a chair. Brent's face turned scarlet. Jevic seldom had the opportunity to witness his witty friend speechless and struggled to keep himself from exploding with laughter when Christina sat down beside him.

Following a couple seconds of awkward silence, Christina asked, "Was this seat taken?"

"No, it's all yours," Jevic replied, leaning back in his seat to enjoy the show. Brent sat frozen beside her.

"I hope you didn't get into any trouble over what happened," she said to Brent. "I saw everything. Those guys were just waiting for the chance to make trouble."

Jevic watched Brent staring vacantly into his plate without saying a word for way too long. He gave him a kick under the table, which was just enough to snap him out of it.

"Uh, no. Principal Lewis was actually very cool about it. And every time Reilly opened his big mouth, he got himself in deeper trouble."

"Good," Christina said with a flirtatious smile.

Jevic raised his eyebrows and grinned from across the table. He knew that Brent had waited a long time for her to notice what a great guy he was.

After Brent's initial shock wore off, his senses returned. "Thanks for talking to the principal. He said you both stopped by his office."

"You're welcome," Heather replied.

"Yes, you are welcome," Christina told him. "It's nice to see someone try to put Reilly in his place, but I think you should stay away from him now."

"It's too late for that," Brent told them. "He's got to defend his wounded pride."

"You can avoid him. Just ignore the creep," Christina suggested.

"People like Reilly don't just let you walk away," Brent argued.

"He's insecure, probably pushed around, or ignored, by his father at home. He tries to bully everyone else to make himself feel superior. Just a product of his environment, like the rest of us," Heather said.

Brent looked across the table at Heather. Where does she come up with these things? He glanced at Jevic, who seemed to know exactly what he was thinking and just shrugged his shoulders.

The conversation turned away from the sore subject of the incident and focused on everyone's vacation plans for the summer. Heather's family had a backpacking trip planned, and Christina was going away to cheerleading camp for two weeks. Brent's family was going to be spending most of their weekends at their camp in the Adirondacks, as they did every summer. Jevic usually spent a lot of time up there too. They loved to hike in the mountains and had plans to climb all of the 46 high peaks.

But now, for the first time, Jevic wondered exactly what this summer would be like for him. Everyone else was going on with their lives, and he had no idea where his would take him. He tried to hide all of the strange things that had been happening in the back of his mind while he was in school. He didn't want his friends, especially Brent, to be suspicious. No one could know about what was going on. He'd have to deal with all that on his own.

Jevic stayed after school that day and was amazed at how much information he was able to find on the Stone of Destiny. It seemed there were several theories about its origin. The first, that it was the stone from which young King Arthur pulled the sword Excalibur. A second theory claimed it was the stone used for Jacob's pillow, as referenced in the Bible.

There were also references of the Tuatha Dé Danann, ancient, mystical people who traveled to Ireland from four islands to the north. According to the information Jevic found, one magical treasure was brought from each of those four islands. Upon their arrival in Ireland, the Tuatha Dé Danann placed the Stone of Destiny on a mound at Tara. Because they were so different from the other people who lived on the island, these strangers were not warmly accepted. Eventually, they were forced to dwell beneath the hills or sidhe, which is how they came to be called the Sidhe.

Jevic was totally amazed to discover the Sidhe were a topic for discussion on the Internet. Although, as King Ronan had mentioned, human references to their existence were usually limited to myths and fairy tales rather than actual accounts of history.

Whatever its origin, there were many stories regarding the history of the Stone, which changed hands many times. In several places, it was stated that the true Stone of Destiny was enchanted and would roar or call out when the next in line to a throne came in contact with it; just as Ronan had claimed. Legend has it that one king, who was unhappy with the Stone's disapproval of his protégé, chopped the Stone in half with his sword. Jevic had to wonder if the Stone had actually demonstrated disapproval with its silence or if it lacked true magical powers altogether, being one of several fakes that were apparently created as decoys.

Another source claimed a portion of the Stone was given to

the King of Munster who installed it at his stronghold, Blarney Castle. That piece, known as the Blarney Stone, is still a popular tourist attraction today.

Over the years, it seems that there was a great deal of skepticism about whether or not the true stone was taken by King Edward I of England as spoils of war with Scotland. Some theories even claim that the one he brought back with him, which was kept under the coronation chair in Westminster Abbey for seven hundred years, was just a sandstone block, formerly used to hold down the cover of the cess-pit at Scone Castle. The legend boasts that someone had swapped a copy for the original knowing that Edward would be looking to claim it as his prize. These counterfeit copies were allegedly created by monks and/or the Knights Templar as a diversion, in an attempt to keep the true Stone of Destiny from falling into the wrong hands.

Jevic was confused by the many theories he'd uncovered, but it seemed he had one thing going for him that others had not; he knew what the Stone really looked like.

Since there were so many contradicting legends and stories, he printed everything out to take home and read later.

As he stood at the printer waiting for his copies, he was startled by a voice behind him, "The Stone of Destiny, huh?"

"Uh, yeah," he answered, looking over his shoulder at an older boy with red hair and freckles.

"My grandfather told me stories about that," he commented.

"Really," Jevic acknowledged, hoping the copies would print faster.

"Are you doing a report or something?" the stranger asked.

"Something like that," Jevic answered.

"I'm Eric."

"Hi. Jevic," he said tersely.

"You know my grandfather might have a book about the Stone. I remember seeing one on the shelf in our den. I can ask if he'd let you borrow it if you'd like," Eric offered.

Jevic didn't know what to say. Perhaps this was fate playing into his hand and he shouldn't turn down the offer. "Sure, that would be great," he answered. "I could use all the information I can get. I'm kinda pressed for time on this one."

"I'll ask if you can borrow it. It shouldn't be a problem. Where's your locker? I'll stop by with it tomorrow before first period," Eric said.

"That's really cool of you. It's down by the Guidance Office, number 8," Jevic answered. Just then the printer stopped, and Jevic snatched his copies out of the tray. "Well, that's it for me. Thanks again."

"Happy to help!" Eric shouted.

Jevic was uneasy about anybody knowing he was interested in the Stone, but who would ever suspect he was trying to recover something like that. Chances are the kid was just trying to be friendly. Then again, he was older, probably a junior or a senior, what would an older guy want to help a younger kid like him for?

His copies were hastily folded in half and stuffed into his backpack. He was probably just being paranoid, but if he could avoid anyone else knowing about this, he was definitely going to.

8 ~ THE BROTHERHOOD ~

Between his workload for school and his research on the lost treasure, Jevic was stuck in the house all evening. He sat in his room reading through everything he had printed, making notes and highlighting points he thought might be significant. Because there were still so many theories, he found himself wishing he had someone to help him weed out the facts. If he could only get a chance to speak with Aaron, perhaps he could shed some light on the truth.

His dad was still upset about the fight at school, so he was happy to have enough work to keep him busy in his room until bedtime. As he lay on his bed, he pulled the medallion out from under his shirt and held it in his hand. The metal was warm from the heat of his body, and the edges incredibly smooth. Turning it over, he once again read the name on the back and wondered about the man who'd worn it before him.

Could he even call him a man? Many of the Sidhe looked like ordinary people but they were definitely different. Everything he'd seen on his trip to their world was evidence of that. The entire place was filled with that brilliant light that didn't come from the sun. Their music, food, artwork and mannerisms were so elaborate and refined. He remembered how effortlessly Aaron was able to change his appearance and how surprised he'd been to look up, instead of down, at him for the first time. He wondered if the king really had the power to read his mind and how he'd projected that image of the Stone into the air.

Jevic slowly rubbed the medallion between his fingertips. It had a definite calming effect on him, and he remembered the worry beads that he'd seen Heather wear on her wrist. She'd probably be the one friend he could talk to about this stuff.

No! I can't let anyone know. It's important that no one else knows. He already regretted that guy Eric finding out, even though he seemed ok. I'll have to be more careful from now on, he thought.

His finger ran repeatedly over the name on the back. A thousand years ago. Did he wear this when he was my age? What kind of a guy was he, and exactly how had he died? Jevic drifted off to sleep while trying to imagine who this man from the Otherworld was, the man who shared his name. How had he lived and how he had died?

Suddenly, he was walking through the woods near the West Brook. A thick fog rolling through the valley made it difficult for him to find his way. As the fog grew denser, he stumbled into a large rock where he decided to sit and wait for the air to clear.

In the distance, he could hear music. It was the same tune he'd heard on his way through the corridor beneath the oak tree. He wished it were louder so he might understand the words that went along with the beautiful melody.

Through the mist a shadow was moving toward him. As it drew closer, Jevic could make out the figure of a tall man with broad shoulders.

"Are you lost, my friend?" the shadowy stranger asked.

"No, Sir, just waiting until I can see more clearly which direction to take," Jevic answered.

"I understand," the stranger told him. "It's easy to become confused, even in a familiar place, when we're faced with an unusual challenge."

"This is very unusual, and I don't want to take a wrong

turn," Jevic admitted.

"It takes courage to move your feet when you're not sure of the way."

"I'm afraid I'll get lost," Jevic confessed.

"Why does that frighten you?" the man asked.

"I may not find my way home again," he said softly.

The man moved closer so that Jevic could see his bearded face and long, curly brown hair. He had crystal blue eyes that seemed to cut through the fog and strong, rugged looking features. He bent down on a knee and looked at him directly.

"This is a big world, Jevic. Anyone can sit safely in one place, but only a chosen few have the courage to step into the unknown and do what we were born to do."

"You know my name?" the boy asked.

"I am the one who whispered it into your mother's ear. I waited a long time to pass my name on. It is a good name, but only a name. It is you who will make your mark, in this world and the other," the stranger told him.

"Are you really?" Jevic asked.

"Prince Jevic of the Sidhe, and you not only bear my name but my medallion as well." The man lifted the golden tree from Jevic's chest and rubbed it slowly between his fingers. "It is no easy task that the world asks of you, but what is life if not a chance to prove yourself useful? You will be the single grain of sand that tips the scale." The man smiled and rested his empty hand on Jevic's shoulder. "Remember, without fear, courage does not exist."

Jevic sat upright in his bed with a gasp. He looked down at his hand closed tightly around the medallion and fell back onto his pillow. Well, that was different, he thought. His heart pounded loudly as he slipped the chain back under his shirt and laid his hand over it.

The next morning Eric showed up at Jevic's locker just as he'd opened it.

"How's it going?" he asked as he leaned against the locker next to Jevic's with one hand and held an old book out in the other.

"Great, you got it!" said Jevic, taking it from him. The title on the cover was barely visible. "Wow, it looks pretty old. Are you sure it's all right if I borrow it?"

"Sure. My grandfather's always happy to see kids using books. He says the electronic age will be the end of us all," Eric chuckled.

"Yeah, my parents worry about that too," Jevic replied.

"Well, be careful not to lose that. You can drop it off at my locker, #212, whenever you're finished with it," Eric told him as he walked away.

"I'll take care of it. Thanks again."

Jevic opened the book's cover and gently turned the first few brittle pages. This thing is ancient, he thought, and he tucked it safely into his backpack.

After school, he escaped to Apple Rock with the book. He was happy to see his beautiful tree waiting in the sunshine by the stream.

"Hey there," he greeted casually.

He leaned his hawthorn staff against the rock and straddled his branch so he could see her face.

"Hello, Jevic. How is everything?" she asked softly.

His immediate answer to that question was usually, "Good," but this time he hesitated. "I really don't know. I'm confused. I'm worried because I have so little time to find the Stone and no clue where to begin," he confided in her.

"Don't worry. You'll figure it out," she reassured. "I'm happy you're here. Is that a school book?" she asked, remembering how he used to sit with her to do his homework.

Jevic held the book up in front of him. "No, it's about the Stone. I borrowed it from a kid at school."

The tree looked concerned.

"Don't worry. I'm not going around telling everyone about this stuff. Some kid saw me printing information and offered to lend me this."

The spirit face on the apple tree softened.

"Hey," Jevic said, "The trees of the Triad had me pick one

of their leaves so I could hear what they were saying. Do you think that will work with you?"

"I don't know. Try, if you wish," she replied.

Jevic noticed one of the few late blossoms still hanging from her branches. He reached for that instead of a leaf and gently plucked it.

"Tell me, who's your favorite guy in the entire world?" he asked, stepping away from the tree with the blossom in hand.

"Brent Thomas is a pretty good kid." He heard her answer clearly, and then she started to laugh.

"Really!" Jevic exclaimed. The sound of her laughter was so beautiful Jevic wished it would go on forever. Hearing it made everything better.

"You know you're my favorite," she confessed.

He pulled the silk pouch from his pocket and slipped the blossom inside. Then he sat on his branch and opened the book. A piece of paper fell from between the pages, and Jevic caught it just before it hit the water.

The paper seemed to groan with age as he unfolded it. It was a letter dated the 20th day of June, 1789. I doubt Eric's grandfather knew this was in here, he thought.

There was a symbol at the top with two knights riding together on one horse. Jevic recognized it from the Internet as a symbol of the Knights Templar. And the letter read:

To our brothers in America:

The brotherhood has agreed it would be prudent to move a certain item, which has been in our possession for some time, to a more remote location due the considerable interest that has been demonstrated in this object.

Since most of the interest in this item has been concentrated here in the Isles, it should be much more secure under your vigilant care in the Colonies. This item will be arriving by ship in Albany on or about the 12th day of August.

Please make the appropriate arrangements for its safe reception at the port and discrete accommodations for its safe keeping.

Peace and good health to you, my brothers.
Grand Master, Kenneth Bartholomew

Jevic couldn't believe what he'd read. Was this a letter regarding the Stone? According to legend, the Knights Templar had claimed to have it under their protection at one time.

While Jevic examined the letter more closely, considering if it could truly be two hundred years old, he failed to notice that Aaron had appeared beside him.

"What are you reading?" he asked, startling Jevic so badly that he nearly fell off of his branch and into the stream.

"What are you trying to do, give me a heart attack?" he shouted.

Aaron was laughing. "You'd better be more alert than that. You never know who might be sneaking up on you. Where is your staff?"

"Good idea! I could have hit you with it," Jevic answered sarcastically.

"Jevic, if I were someone who meant you harm, that staff would have alerted you," Aaron explained.

"What do you mean?"

"It is meant to protect you. If you're in contact with it, the staff will vibrate when an enemy approaches. I should have told you before." Aaron's tone was somewhat apologetic. "I forget you are not familiar with such things."

Jevic looked at the stick leaning against the rock. "It shaped to my hand when I held it," Jevic said.

"It imprinted your energy. It now protects only you."

"Cool," he commented. But he still did not fully appreciate the power of the hawthorn's gift to him.

Aaron was appearing in human size for the first time outside of the Otherworld. The prince had an air of confidence about him that made Jevic feel safe.

"I like you better like this, full-sized," Jevic said. Then he asked, "Can I talk with you about some things?"

Aaron sat on the tree limb beside him, and Jevic shared

with him everything he'd learned about the Stone's history so far.

"Well done," Aaron praised. "How did you learn so much so quickly?"

"I used the Internet," Jevic told him.

Aaron looked confused.

Jevic laughed and his brain scrambled for a way to describe the Web. "It's like another realm," he said. "People go there to share information and thoughts with each other using machines, called computers, to communicate."

"Interesting," Aaron said, "Can you be sure the information is correct?"

"Not really. You have to trust the people who share it," Jevic said.

"Did you find this letter when you were in the Internet realm?" Aaron asked.

Jevic tried not to laugh and was happy he'd used the word Internet because "Web" could have really caused confusion. "No. I got the letter from a boy at school."

"You told him?" Aaron asked with a tone of extreme concern.

"No, no," Jevic tried to explain, but Aaron interrupted.

"You must be cautious about trusting people, Jevic," he warned. "Not everyone is worthy."

The boy conceded. "I know. Normally, I wouldn't trust a stranger, but this letter tells that something, possibly the Stone, was shipped here over two hundred years ago. Maybe I was supposed to meet this guy. You know? Maybe it's all a part of my destiny."

"My father had visions that the Stone was within your reach," Aaron told him.

"If that's what this letter is talking about, it really may be within my reach," Jevic justified enthusiastically.

The prince's expression was very serious as he warned, "Be very careful, Jevic. The Stone of Destiny belongs to my people, but there are many others who would have it...at any cost."

81

9 ~ STARLIGHT ~

Jevic found Eric in school the next morning. He pulled the old book out of his backpack and handed it to the boy.

Eric smiled and said, "Finished already? Did you find anything interesting?"

"Yeah, a couple of things," Jevic answered.

"Good," Eric told him. "You never know what you'll find in an old book like this."

There was still something about this kid that made Jevic uneasy. "No, you don't," he agreed. Then he asked, "How old is your grandfather anyway?"

"Older than dirt," Eric answered. "He talks about the old country all of the time; he was born and raised in Ireland."

"My great-grandmother was too," Jevic said.

"When he gets going, it seems like he's talking about an entirely different world. I sometimes wonder if he's gone a bit nutty in his old age," the older boy said. "But then, to hear some of the stories he tells about when he was younger makes me wonder if he was always nutty."

Jevic was determined to figure out what it was that he didn't trust about this guy, and he suddenly realized he was staring awkwardly, which seemed to make Eric noticeably uncomfortable.

So Jevic threw his backpack over one shoulder and said, "Well, thanks again."

Don't mention it," Eric mumbled. Then, he called out, "Oh, there's one more thing my grandfather said. If anyone really wanted to learn the secrets of that Stone, they'd find them in the stars."

"The stars?" Jevic repeated.

"I told you, he's nutty as a squirrel turd," Eric laughed.

Jevic smiled as he turned to walk down the hall. Or maybe crazy like a fox, he thought. What if there was a group of people who were trying to keep the Stone out of the wrong hands until they could find a way to get it back where it belonged. If fate placed people in places just so they'd cross paths, maybe that old man had been waiting for someone to borrow his book. Maybe he even knew about the letter inside of it. A kid who was just working on a report wouldn't give a second thought to a crazy old man who talked to himself, but a guy who was able to talk to trees and elemental spirits would take notice.

If I'm right, I just got a nudge in the right direction. I'm not sure exactly what I'm looking for, but if the sky is clear tonight, I'll start by looking up.

That night at dinner, Jevic told his parents he wanted to go outside and watch for shooting stars. "Dad, do you think I could borrow your telescope?" he asked.

His dad had owned a telescope since his days at college when he took astronomy class, but now, it just sat in the closet. "Sure, Jev," he answered enthusiastically. "Might be a good idea to dust that thing off and see if it still works."

Jevic and his father had always been close, but since the fight he'd gotten into at school, Jevic had noticed a chill in their relationship. He didn't like the cold shoulder treatment his dad had been giving him lately, but honestly, he didn't have much time to worry about things like that now. He knew his dad would eventually get over it, but he didn't expect it would happen tonight when he really didn't want it to.

"Want me to show you how to use it?" his father offered

with the same tone he used when Jevic needed help with math or science. His dad was a very smart guy, but he had a tendency to make a big deal out of stuff like this.

Jevic stared desperately into his mashed potatoes in search of an answer. The two of them hadn't spent much time together lately. But Jevic had no idea what he was looking for, and time was something of a rare commodity at the moment. Nevertheless, when he looked up and saw the excitement on his father's face, he had no choice. "Sure, that would be great!" he answered.

Since their house was surrounded by woods, the only place clear enough to set up the scope was the small open lawn on the west side. His dad enthusiastically showed him how to adjust the lens and then spent several minutes getting the moon perfectly focused.

"There you go, Jev. Have a look at that beauty. Careful, don't touch anything. Just look down into the eyepiece," he told him. "I have it focused perfectly."

Jevic, who had been combing the heavens with his sharp, young eyes while his dad fussed with the telescope, bent down and carefully looked into the eyepiece. "It's a little blurry, Dad," he said.

His father pulled his glasses off. "Let me see," he said, taking another peek. "Looks perfect to me."

"Maybe I need to adjust it for my own eyes," Jevic suggested as he watched his father slip his glasses back onto his nose.

"Oh, right. The last time I used this with my college buddies we all had 20/20 vision. Turn this until it's focused," he instructed, pointing to a knob on the side.

"Yeah, that's better," Jevic commented.

His father tried to look again, but now it was completely out of focus for him. "Well," he said with a grin, "That's what the moon looks like. There's no sense in the two of us trying to refocus that darn thing all night long. You go ahead and use it. Here, you'll need this too."

He pulled a book from the same bag that had stored the

telescope and showed Jevic a map of the constellations on the inside cover. "I left it out under the lamp in the living room for a while. I can't believe it still works," he said proudly.

As Jevic opened the cover, he was thoroughly impressed when he realized the map was printed in ink that glowed in the dark. The constellations were so clearly visible that he needed no flashlight to see them.

"Thanks Dad," he said, "This is awesome!"

His father smiled proudly as he pointed out the Big Dipper, both in the book and in the sky. "That should get you started," he said. "I'm sure you'll figure the rest out for yourself."

Jevic gave his father a hug, a real hug, not one of those quick, awkward ones he'd been giving him since he'd been tall enough to look him in the eye.

The significance of this gesture did not go unnoticed. "Don't stay up all night, Jev," his father cautioned with a bit of emotion stuck in his throat. "Remember, you have school in the morning."

"I won't," his boy promised with a smile.

Jevic watched his dad walk back into the house. Then he focused his attention on the book in his hands. It took him a minute or two to coordinate the telescope with the stars overhead, but he finally had the Big Dipper in his sights. Ursa Major, he read beneath the constellation on the page. Yeah, I remember that from science class, he thought. He also knew there was a Little Dipper and searched the map for a smaller version until he found it. It was upside down and opposite the other as if the little one was pouring into the larger.

The only constellation separating the two was Draco. It appeared that the tail of this dragon shaped group of stars ran right between Ursa Major and Ursa Minor. Polaris, the North Star, was a bright star at the tip of the Little Dipper's handle.

Being a hiker, Jevic knew that the North Star was the one people looked for to find their way under the night sky. Guess that's as good a place to start as any, he thought.

He looked first at the sky and then through the scope, slowly moving it in the direction of Ursa Minor until he had

Polaris perfectly centered in the field of vision. Now what, he wondered as he examined the star through the eyepiece. What am I seriously expecting to find anyway? Jevic sat down in the dewy grass with a sigh and leaned back on his elbows to think.

I think there are more stars now than there were five minutes ago. I think that maybe I'm grasping at straws here. And I think I probably should have been named George or something because I'm just not convinced that this whole destiny thing is working out for me. What am I going to do? How can I tell Aaron he must have the wrong guy, and…what the heck is that?

A shooting star was moving across the northern sky toward Polaris. Just as it was about to cross in front of the North Star, it disappeared in a brilliant flash. Jevic jumped to his feet and scrambled for the telescope. The North Star was still centered perfectly and looked exactly as it had before. Was that just a coincidence? He stepped away from the tripod supporting the telescope and looked up at the star in the sky again.

Suddenly, there was another flash and a circle of six stars appeared around Polaris. They began to rotate clockwise. After one complete rotation, the star at the top of the ring broke out of formation and the others followed in a sparkling string of light.

His eyes were glued to the tiny lights as they seemed to descend from the sky in his direction with incredible speed. He drew a deep breath and held it as he watched these lights moving closer and closer. Their straight path changed to a spiral, wrapping back into a ring in the air right above his head. He exhaled and gulped in another breath but never took his eyes off of the six lights as they moved within their circular path, slower and slower until they completely stopped their rotation and hung in the air only ten feet away. Now each light was about the size of a baseball and resembled a dried dandelion flower; a semi-transparent globe seemingly made up of many small beams of light projected from a small, dark inner sphere. Although he was terrified, Jevic couldn't help being impressed with these incredibly beautiful orbs.

As he watched the lights in utter amazement, they began to move closer together in their circular formation. The ring grew smaller and smaller until the six orbs were nearly touching each other, and once again they began to spin while pulsing softly in perfect unison. It was hypnotic, so much so that Jevic didn't even notice the orbs were gradually closing in as they pulsated faster. They were an arm's length away from his face when he heard an airy voice whisper, "If you are the one, then follow us."

Without any hint of a warning, there was a magnificent explosion that threw Jevic backwards into the tripod, knocking the telescope to the ground. He struggled to focus his eyes after the flash. The six orbs had apparently multiplied in number, now a swarm of smaller orbs swirled over the yard like a small galaxy moving gracefully in a giant sweeping spiral across the night sky.

Just as unexpectedly, there was a second explosion. This time, the spiraling swarm had multiplied inconceivably and scattered tiny lights throughout the woods like a million fireflies. They were everywhere, countless twinkling little lights. It gave Jevic the remarkable feeling that every single star had fallen from the heavens to the earth around him.

And in the midst of all this, his mind struggled. Am I the one? What do I do, he asked himself, follow them? How do I follow them? They're everywhere, he panicked, everywhere. He took one step toward the forest and fear grabbed hold of him. What might be waiting for him out there in the darkness, in his woods?

Remembering Aaron's warning Jevic ran back and grabbed the hawthorn staff he'd left leaning against the side of their old stone house. He didn't know what kind of protection a stick would be, but that was all he had.

10 ~ DARKNESS ~

Jevic's fingers tightened around the hawthorn staff as he left the starlit sky behind and stepped under the canopy of the trees. Rather than the darkness he'd expected, the woods were illuminated with the mysterious little lights scattered from ground to treetop as far as his eyes could see. He was surrounded.

They're just like fireflies, he told himself, but even this voice of reason inside of his head seemed to be trembling. While trying to gather his wits, he awaited direction.

Ok, you wanted me to follow you; now what, that inner voice asked?

As if responding to his thoughts, the lights began to rain down from the treetops and sweep toward him from every direction. In a matter of seconds, thousands, maybe millions, of tiny lights had formed a glowing corridor that stretched from where he was standing to deep in the forest.

Jevic drew a slow, ragged breath and began to walk along the lighted path before him. He was trying very hard not to let himself imagine what was waiting at the other end. But with each step, something was gnawing at his gut, telling him not to underestimate the power of these strange lights. His grip around the hawthorn branch tightened.

These brilliant walls of light, which seemed to be moving along with him, made it difficult for Jevic to see anything else in the woods. He wished he could catch a glimpse of the tree faces and read their expressions. However, even those closest to him were nothing more than undefined shadows in the darkness.

As he slowly made his way along the path, he questioned his decision to continue with every step.

"If you are the one, then follow us," the orb had said. Why did I? Jevic asked himself. Why didn't I just go inside and go to bed? I didn't even consider it. Maybe I am the one, and somehow deep down in my soul I know it, he thought.

Like a mouse in a maze, he was led down the hillside in the direction of the West Brook. He could hear the familiar sound of the water, and his feet recognized every root and patch of dirt beneath them. Although this familiarity was only mildly reassuring, he began to pick up his pace.

Jevic was heading downhill parallel to the stream when he heard something in the woods to his right that made him stop short. His eyes widened. His ears strained, and his fingers squeezed hard into their impressions on the motionless staff. Holding completely still, he waited for the slightest movement in the darkness, but the entire forest was as motionless as the staff in his hand.

After a minute or so, he decided to continue. Perhaps it was just a…There it was again! Something was moving toward him. Jevic held the hawthorn out in front of him and turned in the direction of the noise. He could hear its breath and feel the force of its feet against the ground as it leapt onto the path in front of him. The wide-eyed doe, terrified by the strange lights, barely touched ground before she vanished into the darkness on the other side.

Jevic felt foolish for not recognizing that doe. He knew her when she was a fawn two years ago. He knew where she bedded down at night, and he'd heard her footsteps countless times in these woods.

I'm letting these lights freak me out. I need to get a hold of myself.

He took a few deep breaths and moved on toward a large oak that the lights had completely surrounded. As he got closer, even the lights that were behind him flowed past the young Seer toward that tree. By the time he reached the oak's trunk, it was as bright as daylight beneath it.

As Jevic walked a full circle around the old giant, the first thing he noticed was that it had no face. He knew this tree. Over the past few years, it had shown little sign of life. Leaves had only grown on one or two of its hundreds of branches. But now, he realized it must be dead. Why had they led him here?

Before he'd finished that thought, the air began to stir and the lights moved into a formation that resembled a long glowing tube. It twisted swiftly and gracefully around the great tree again and again; coiling itself loosely around it like an enormous snake. Jevic backed slowly against the trunk as the snake began to constrict. His grip tightened around the still motionless staff he was holding straight out in front of him. Wasn't this thing supposed to protect me?

The scent of burning wood filled the air as the coil worked its way into the branches above his head. Jevic closed his eyes to its blinding light. Within seconds there was a searing pain in his outstretched hand that forced him to cry out. He jerked his hand back and pressed his body firmly against the oak with his outstretched arms wrapped tightly against the trunk to either side. The fingers on his right hand dug desperately into the old bark as the scorching coil closed painfully in on him.

The blistering heat gouged brutally into his face. Jevic struggled to think, but he had only one thought—there is no way out. He could smell the heat and see the blinding light clearly through his closed eyes. Would the last thing he'd ever smell be his own burning hair? It was too much to bear; the heat, the pain. He couldn't even breathe. His right hand searched desperately for something to hang on to, something that would anchor him to life and not let him slip away. There was a bump, a knot on the side of the tree the size and shape of a door knob. It fit perfectly into his right hand that clung to it like life itself. Jevic could feel his skin baking and thought his clothes must surely be on fire but dared not open his eyes.

"God, help me," Jevic prayed. He squeezed the knot as he drew what surely would be his last breath, and it turned. He felt the tree breaking away behind him and stumbled backward into total darkness.

He gasped another unexpected breath. "Holy hell!" he panted in wide-eyed blindness. "Where am I?"

Was he inside of the tree? Jevic reached out to feel his way through the darkness around him. The knuckles on his left hand brushed against a wall of some sort sending a burning pain screaming up his arm. He dropped to his knees and cradled his hand close to his chest as his eyes begged for some sign of light.

He called out desperately, "Hello...can anyone hear me?" His voice echoed off into the darkness, but there was no answer.

It wasn't so much the darkness that bothered him as it was the lack of light; he needed to see where he was. This was the most complete darkness he'd ever experienced. Were his eyes even open? What if that light blinded me? Jevic tried to imagine what that would be like; never again seeing the blue of the sky, or the view from a mountaintop, or the faces of people he loves.

Then a fear that was even more horrible entered his thoughts—maybe I'm dead!

He was a heartbeat away from total panic when reason spoke. Wait! You can't be dead. Your hand wouldn't hurt. When a smile started to spread across his face, he realized that it hurt too, worse than any sunburn he could ever imagine. But things were looking up—at least he wasn't dead.

Jevic pulled himself onto his feet and patted his hand against his thigh to feel what he had in his pockets. There was the silk pouch. He pressed his hand against it and called out again, "Can anyone hear me?" His words echoed off again with no reply. Frantically he searched the other pocket. There were a couple of quarters, a hall pass, and a pack of gum. If he were like most other guys his age, he'd have a lighter in his pocket.

His right hand reached out to locate the wall behind him and leaned his head back against it to think. What were those lights? Why did they lead me here? Why would they try to fry me alive and then leave me alone in this place? I wish Aaron was here. I wish I had a rag and lighter so I could make this useless staff into a torch. I wish...I wish I was home in bed and that my parents had named me George.

He felt his lower lip twitch and his eyes welled up. Why shouldn't I cry? Was there ever anyone with a better reason than this?

His thoughts were interrupted by a flicker of light that broke through the darkness in front of him. Jevic blinked hard and watched as the tiny spark grew quickly into an orb. No, not again, he pleaded. He held very still against the wall.

Well, at least I'm not blind, he reassured himself.

Then the same airy voice he'd heard from the orb before spoke again. "You are the one. Only the chosen one could have opened the door."

Jevic didn't say a word, didn't breathe. He stood silently against the inside of the hollow tree as his eyes surveyed his surroundings in the dim light the orb was casting. The weak glow washed over the walls of a small cylindrical space. He must be inside of the tree. Despite his effort to go unnoticed, the sphere seemed aware of his exact location within the cramped space. It pulsed slowly as if waiting for him to respond.

When he accepted that there was no ignoring this thing, he demanded, "What do you want?"

"To meet you," it whispered.

"How neighborly," Jevic mumbled sarcastically.

"You have been tested," the voice informed him. "Now, they will meet you."

"Who?"

"The king and queen," the orb replied. "You will follow

me."

"I've already met them," the boy argued. But the orb did not respond.

Jevic tried to make sense of what was going on. Why would the king send these things to test him like this? Didn't he already trust him? Did Aaron know about this? His head was reeling with crazy, confusing questions. Had he no other option but to follow that damned light again?

The orb grew brighter before drifting into a small dark tunnel near the ground on the opposite side of the round space. Jevic brushed his hair back away from his face and watched the orb floating eerily away. He gave the hawthorn staff a squeeze and stooped low to keep from hitting his head as he stepped into the musty-smelling corridor. It couldn't have been more different than the first time he'd been led underground to meet the king and queen. Where was he going? Turning back to look at the black place behind him, he knew he had no choice but to follow this haunting light.

He walked for several minutes, at a rapid rate of descent. The walls were dripping with liquid that smelled like the unidentifiable moldy stuff he'd occasionally find in the back of their fridge. The stench was nauseating and he found himself fighting the urge to gag. Remembering the gum in his pocket, he slipped a piece into his mouth to mask the odor and settle his stomach. No further words were exchanged between the orb and the Seer until they reached the end of the tunnel.

The kingdom of the Sidhe, where he was taken before, had been nothing like this place. It was dark and seemingly lifeless here. The dull glow of twilight stretched along the horizon, and hundreds of orbs, like the one guiding him, were scattered randomly across the countryside. There was no singing or dancing in this place, no smell of flowers on the wind that moaned through the lifeless trees flanking the muddy road before him.

"What is this place?" Jevic asked.

"The Otherworld," the orb answered.

"I've been there, and it didn't look like this," he argued.

"This is the kingdom of the Unseelie Court," the orb informed him.

"But you said you were taking me to meet the king and…"

Suddenly, he realized what was happening. He swallowed hard, and his gum went down. But that wasn't the largest lump in his throat. He'd been captured by the enemy, the enemy who had killed Prince Jevic. How could he escape? He only knew one way out, and he was in no hurry to get back to the barbecue.

As he took a reluctant step out of the tunnel, the hawthorn staff began to shake. Now it warns me, he thought. And with each step, the vibrations grew stronger. There were faint human-like shadows in the distance. Although they did not approach him, they did follow slowly along, parallel to his path. The more he became aware of these shadowy figures, the stronger the staff shook.

Ahead in the darkness, the drooping shadow of a structure stood forebodingly on a rocky hilltop, and the orb moved quickly in its direction. Although he was not at all anxious to meet the head of this place, he was growing increasingly concerned about the multitude of shadowy beings that were quickly gathering around him, and he struggled to keep up.

They passed beneath a great looming arch made of colorless stone with sharp finials hanging from it, like stalactites, into what he would guess was a courtyard. Now the staff shook so violently that he had to carry it with both hands. His eyes climbed a set of cold stone steps up to a pair of thrones that mockingly resembled the ones at the Seelie Court. He remembered how his knees had wobbled as he climbed those gleaming steps. But now, in this place, he couldn't feel his legs at all and wondered again if he might already be dead.

He followed the orb to the top of the steps where it stopped and hovered three feet from the ground before the two thrones.

Upon this pair of unsightly thrones sat a pale, gray couple dressed in dingy, black robes. The king was very tall with beady, red eyes that glowed inside deep, hollow sockets. His jet black hair was wildly unkempt and a mangy beard grew in patches on his face. Long, black fingernails, resembling claws, clicked hauntingly on the arm of his chair as he smiled, a frightening yellow-toothed smile, and Jevic's right knee hit the stone floor.

He honestly didn't know if his leg had just given out or something had forced it down to the ground before these horrible creatures. But Jevic kept his head low and closed his eyes, hoping that when he opened them again he'd be home in his bed.

And then, the airy voice of the orb spoke again. "This is the one," it announced.

Jevic opened his eyes just enough to see his staff vibrating as it lay across his left thigh.

"What is your name?" the king's voice moved across the room like a cold winter wind.

Jevic lifted his head and looked directly into the eyes of the Unseelie ruler.

"George. Say George," a little voice in his head begged. But when the young Seer opened his mouth, "I'm Jevic," clearly came out.

"Jevic," the king's voice echoed, as if coming up from the bottom of an empty well. "Interesting," he said. "You seek the Stone of Destiny?"

"Yes, Sir...Sire," Jevic answered through the sweaty curls in front of his face.

"Why?" the king demanded in a condescending tone.

Jevic searched for the right answer in his terrified mind. "Because King Ronan asked me to," he replied.

"What makes you think you can recover the Stone?" the king spat at the boy as if this exchange of words was leaving a putrid taste in his mouth.

"King Ronan thinks I can find it," Jevic replied instantly. "I promised him I would try."

The king snorted. "The mud on your feet is worth more than that promise, human."

The staff in his lap began to feel warm, shaking constantly

now rather than in pulses. He held it tightly with both hands and prayed silently for a way out of there.

"Tell me," the king spat, "Why would Ronan need help from a filthy human, like you?"

That same question had been lurking in the back of Jevic's mind. How did he end up in this horrible place? He just wanted to be back in his woods surrounded by the beautiful trees. He couldn't bear to think of his home or the Seelie kingdom becoming anything like this. And for the first time in his life, Jevic understood why evil was necessary; it's there for perspective. The choices it forces upon us are what make us who we are; for better or for worse.

Something inside the terrified young man exploded past his fear. Jevic lifted his head and rose to his feet defiantly. If this horrible king wanted to know why he sought the Stone of Destiny, he'd tell him. "I don't want the rest of the world to become dark and disgusting," he dropped his voice very slightly with his final few words, "like this place."

The gray creature on the throne appeared more inspired than insulted. Leaning forward, he focused intensely upon the young man. "This is exactly what your species is doing to the world above. Their arrogant, selfish behavior is a disease that threatens all life on this planet. No other beings pose such a threat, or leave such a path of destruction in their wake. Mankind's inordinate fascination with itself, its total disregard for that which it is a part, strengthens the very darkness that will swallow them up."

Jevic suddenly became disoriented. He steadied himself, his staff planted firmly against the stone floor, as a series of disturbing images flashed rapidly inside his head; mountains of garbage, dead animals on oil-covered beaches, blazing forests, lifeless lakes, six-lane highways, smoggy city skylines, and then, a mushroom cloud so realistic that its impact left him off balance and gasping for a breath.

"Stop!" Jevic shouted. "You're wrong. People won't allow Earth to become another lifeless planet. I won't allow it." Then he pounded the base of his staff against the stone floor. Maybe it was just for effect. Maybe it was just because he was angry and scared and wanted to hit something. Or maybe it was fate guiding his hand. The motivation didn't matter because the effect was undoubtedly impressive. A blinding light erupted from the top of his staff, bouncing laser-like beams off every surface in the great, gray hall.

Jevic momentarily misinterpreted the overwhelming display of force as an attack aimed at him, and jumped with a start. Obviously, there was a little more to this staff than he'd realized. But was it scaring anybody else? He stood a little taller and lifted his chin.

The king's red eyes glowed like hot coals in their sockets as the energy in the room seemed to rise up like a giant wave about to come crashing down upon the young man.

Jevic brazenly addressed the king again, "If you have no further questions for me, Sire, I'll be going now."

"You worthless, insolent, filthy HUMAN!" the king bellowed. "You will never leave here alive!"

Jevic's blood ran like ice through his veins as loving memories of his parents, Alicia and Brent flashed in his mind's eye. Is this it then, he wondered? Will anyone ever know what happened to me? It will kill Mom if I don't come home. I can't die here, he thought as the king's words echoed hauntingly in the darkness, "...never leave here alive!"

"Like I said, I'll be going n..." Jevic was interrupted by an intense pressure around his upper arms, which was followed by the most overwhelming pain he'd ever experienced. Such pain would have justified a blood-curdling scream, but there was no breath as waves of convulsive response possessed him. The darkness was swallowing him up, and he was completely powerless against it. As his knees hit the floor, the room was flooded with a brief but blinding light that left Aaron standing beside him on the cold stone floor.

The Seelie Prince bent one knee and bowed his head. "King Magnus," he said respectfully. "I ask your permission to speak on this young man's behalf."

"You're too late, Aaron. He has insulted my kingdom, and

he will be punished," Magnus hissed.

Only semi-conscious, Jevic realized the pain, for the most part, had stopped. He turned his head enough to see the shadow of a hand clamped around his left bicep and made a feeble attempt to break free as the Seelie Prince rose to his feet.

With the cool tone of a seasoned diplomat, Aaron stated calmly, "You cannot harm him, Sire."

"Cannot? You dare tell me what I cannot do?" the king roared, and the ground beneath them shook.

"Jevic O'Connor is my father's ambassador brought here by your invitation. As such, he is protected by the diplomatic rights of Sidhe law," Aaron explained. Then, bending close to the young Seer, he whispered, "Show him your medallion."

Jevic jerked his arm free from whatever was holding him and lifted the precious disk out into the light radiating from his staff on the ground in front of him.

"NO!" the king's voice rolled like a storm through the halls and across the dark lands beyond.

With no apparent reaction to the royal outburst, Aaron stated, "I have come to escort him back to my father."

"You have not seen the last of me, boy," the king threatened. "We will meet again and finish what we've started here."

"I look forward to that, Sire," Jevic remarked boldly as he retrieved the hawthorn branch from the ground.

Aaron promptly laid a hand on his shoulder, and instantly, they were in the center of the golden tree in the Seelie courtyard. He dropped to the ground and grabbed Jevic by the shoulders. "Are you all right?" his voice trembled.

Exhausted, Jevic nodded and dropped his forehead against Aaron's shoulder. "I've never been so happy to see anyone," he breathed.

The prince pulled Jevic against his chest and exhaled, "Now try to tell me I've got the wrong guy."

11 ~ LIES ~

From the edge of the woods, Aaron watched Jevic walk back through his yard and pick up the telescope that was lying in the wet grass. He waited until young man had stepped safely inside of the stone house before he vanished into the forest.

It was quiet inside. Jevic had never been so thankful to be home, and thankful his family had apparently gone to bed. He dried off the telescope and he slipped it back into its bag along with his father's book. As he zipped the bag closed, he realized how badly his left hand was burned. It seemed looking at it made it even more painful.

He shoved the telescope into the closet. "If I never look through that thing again, it will be too soon," he mumbled.

All Jevic wanted to do was crawl into bed, but he'd walked over to the sink and was running cool water over his hand when he heard the door to Alicia's room open behind him. He turned the faucet off and quickly grabbed a towel.

"Are ya just getting in from your star gazing?" she asked in a whisper. But when he turned to face her, the old woman gasped. "What'n hell happened to you?"

"What do you mean?" he countered, adjusting the towel to cover his hand completely.

"Your face is scarlet," she answered.

Jevic rushed over to the mirror by the door to look at his reflection.

"Oh, no," he groaned. He looked like a steamed lobster. He'd been in such pain with the burn on his hand that he hadn't thought about what the rest of him looked like.

Alicia appeared beside him in the mirror. "Give me that towel," she said, "I'll soak it in cool water for you." With no more warning than that, she pulled it away from him.

"Owww!" he howled.

"Sweet mother of God," she whispered. Her green eyes instantly welled with sympathetic tears. "Jev, what happened to you? Look at your hand."

Jevic just stared at her. He didn't know what to say. He couldn't lie and didn't want to worry her. So there wasn't much of the truth that he could share.

He finally answered honestly, "I can't tell you."

The look of concern in Alicia's eyes was more painful than his burns, and he felt horrible denying her an explanation.

"I wish I could. I wish I could tell someone, but I can't," he added in a quivering voice.

"Sit down here," Alicia told him. She pulled a chair out from the kitchen table, and he collapsed into it. Holding his head in his hands, elbows on the table, he waited quietly as his grandmother brought cool cloths for his burns.

"Put this on your face, and let me have a look at that hand," she ordered. "Good Lord. What burned you like this?"

He pulled the towel away and peeked at her with a pleading eye.

"I know, you can't talk about it," she snapped impatiently. "Well they are right nasty burns ya have on yur hand. You'll be need'n some'thin to help'em heal."

Her Irish brogue always came back when she was upset like this. Jevic loved to hear it though and in some subtle way it made things seem a little better.

Jevic sat at the table with his face buried in the cool towel as she gathered first aid supplies from the cabinet in the bathroom. It didn't take long for his skin to warm up the towel, but he kept it over his face anyway. It was better than having to look her in the eye. Besides, he didn't want to ask her to rinse it again. He could hear her shuffling across the floor and knew that she wasn't her usual self.

"These look like the electrical burns that yur father once had. That man shouldn't be playing with wires. Just don't have a knack for it," she said.

As she lifted his hand from the table, he peeked over the towel again.

"Keep that on there," she scolded.

He didn't bother arguing and pushed the damp cotton cloth back against his skin. He'd rather not watch anyway. She blotted his hand completely dry with a clean towel and gently spread cool ointment over his fingers and the top of his hand. He tried not to flinch and bit the inside of his cheeks to keep from screaming out and upsetting her any more than she already was. He was grateful when she was finally wrapping it in gauze and he heard the cover snap back onto the roll of adhesive tape.

"Now, let's have a look at that face," Alicia said.

As her fingers gently brushed the curls away from her grandson's forehead, Alicia wondered what kind of legacy she'd handed down to her wonderful boy.

"Well, compared to your hand, I guess this isn't so bad after all," she reported with an agonizing smile.

Jevic watched her squeeze the juice out of a fresh aloe leaf from the plant on the windowsill and tenderly applied the cooling gel to his burns.

As he closed his eyes, enjoying the instant, cooling relief, the young man realized for the first time how lucky he was to have escaped with just a few burns. He was glad that he had Alicia there to help him and wished he didn't have to keep the truth from the only person in his world with any idea what he'd been through.

"Did that cool ya down any?" she asked.

"Yes, thank you. It's a lot better," he said with a stiff smile. "That stuff feels like snot, but I don't care."

"I know exactly wha'cha mean. Makes ya wonder what the first person to try this on a burn was think'in, hey?" Alicia chuckled.

She sat back in her chair and looked lovingly at the young man in front of her. He saw her beautiful eyes welling up again.

"It's ok. I'm ok, Alicia. Please don't cry," he pleaded.

"It was them, wasn't it?" she asked.

Jevic looked down at his bandaged hand and didn't answer.

"I told ya they were right nasty lil boogers," Alicia said, her voice was shaking and a tear escaped down her cheek.

"Not all of them," Jevic argued. "But I definitely met the ones you warned me about tonight." Then he stopped himself before he said too much.

"Did they come look'in for ya?"

Jevic hadn't had a chance to think about that yet. He rewound the chain of events leading up to this night in his head. Who was that Eric kid? Did he think that he could get away with setting him up like this?

"No, they tricked me into looking for them," he answered.

Alicia put her hands over her face and began to cry.

"Please, don't," Jevic begged. "It's really ok. I'm not alone in this thing. There are good people that will stand by me and protect me, like Aaron did tonight. He was there when I didn't think anyone on Earth could save…" Jevic stopped himself in midsentence. He'd said too much.

Jevic pulled Alicia's hands away from her face and onto the table with a gentle squeeze. "You were right," he told her. "I didn't believe it until tonight, but you were right. Destiny does have a plan for me, and I can't ignore it." He squeezed her hand again. "You have always been a part of it too. You taught me so much that no one else could have." Jevic eyes began to blur and he blinked hard. "Every walk we took, every talk we ever had has prepared me for this. You've made me into this person the Seelies believe in. What's expected of me isn't going to be easy. But trust me, you wouldn't want to see the alternative I had a glimpse of tonight."

Jevic glanced at his hand and then back at his grandmother.

"I'm not going to say I'm looking forward any of this. I'm afraid," he swallowed hard. "...afraid I won't be able to do what I have to," he confessed. "But I'm not afraid to try."

"Oh, Jev," Alicia sobbed. "God bless yur heart."

Jevic smiled and kissed her on the cheek. Then he grabbed his staff from beside the door and headed for the stairs to his room. "Oh, don't you ever underestimate that hawthorn cane of yours...something else I learned tonight," he said with a smile.

The next morning Jevic avoided his parents as he dashed out the door to catch the school bus. He hadn't had time to come up with a good excuse for the burns yet and knew they'd demand one. He hadn't thought about an explanation for Brent either, until he sat down beside him on the bus.

"Jeez Louise! What happened to you?" Brent asked.

Jevic stalled with, "What are you talking about?"

"Don't be an idiot," Brent scoffed. "How did your face get burned like that? Did you fall asleep with your head in the microwave?"

Jevic laughed. "Yeah, how'd you guess?"

"Really, Jev, what happened?"

Jevic hated lying more than lima beans, especially to his best friend. "I was burning a pile of brush, and it kinda flared up on me. Stupid accident, that's all," he improvised while avoiding direct eye contact.

Brent had been Jevic's best friend since kindergarten and instantly detected the lie, but best pals don't pry. If Jevic wasn't telling him the truth, then he had a good reason for it. "Huh. That stinks. Got your hand too?" he asked.

"Yeah. I'll be fine," Jevic told him. "I'll know better the next time. Once burned, twice shy–right?"

When Jevic got to school he headed straight for Eric's locker. "I'll catch you later," he told Brent. "I've got something I have to do." He didn't know who that guy was or where he'd come from, but he was going to find out.

Jevic rounded the corner by the gym and followed the hall to where Eric's locker was supposed to be. It was still early, and there was nobody around. He didn't even know the kid's last name or what grade he was in. *Maybe I can find a paper or book with his name on it*, he thought as he stood in front of locker 212.

Jevic lifted the latch, and it opened. But the locker was empty, completely empty. *I knew there was something about that guy that wasn't right*, he told himself, while wishing he'd learn to trust that gut instinct he so often ignored.

He gave the locker door an angry slam that echoed down the empty hallway, but mockingly, the door bounced open again. As he clenched his fist to nail it a second time, he noticed something written on the inside of the door. "If you're reading this, you're better than I expected. Now things will get very interesting."

Jevic slammed the door and landed a solid punch just below the number plate. Who was this jerk? Could he have been one of the Unseelies in disguise? He must have been. Who else would set him up like that? Was that letter even real? It sure looked real. Actually, it was "finding the answer in the stars" that had set him up. The book and letter were probably authentic bait that he used.

What a sucker I am, Jevic thought. *Fell right into that creep's plan and let him try to kill me.* He realized how close Eric had come to doing just that, and a chill ran down his spine. *I'll know better the next time*, he promised himself. *From now on, I can't trust anyone but the people I know. No more strangers.* Then a terrifying idea crossed his mind. *What if they could take the shape of someone he trusted?* No way, he reasoned. *I'd be able to tell, wouldn't I?*

Jevic walked down the hall with his bandaged hand in his pocket where he kept it for most of the day, except when he needed to write. It was a painful reminder of how he must be more careful. Besides, he was tired of everybody asking what had happened. It was bad enough having to lie to Brent, but he had to repeat the same lie over at least a dozen times before lunch.

Lunch came, and for the first time in as long as Brent had

known him, Jevic was not hungry. "What's the matter, Jev?" he asked.

"Think I lost my appetite. Maybe my stomach finally got full," he joked.

Brent smiled. "Don't worry, I'm sure you ate enough yesterday to hold you over."

Jevic grinned and pushed his tray away.

"I'll take that if you're just going to waste it," Brent offered.

"Sure," Jevic said. He wondered if the sick feeling in his gut was partially because he'd been lying all morning. His hand was sore, really sore, and he didn't feel like hanging around school when he had more important things to take care of.

"It could be your burns making you feel lousy," Brent told him. "Remember when I got sun poisoning last year at camp? I felt bad for two days."

"Yeah, that's probably it," Jevic agreed.

"Does it hurt?"

"My face is just tight, but my hand bothers me a bit," he admitted.

Jevic watched Brent swallow a hot dog in two bites. Impressive! Was it really possible? Could someone possibly impersonate his best friend and get away with it? How could he make sure that never happened? He had to find a way to identify the one person he trusted most in the world.

Jevic watched Brent down another hot dog and chug a chocolate milk. I'll bet that Eric guy can't eat like he can, but it wasn't likely that if he showed up again it would be for lunch.

A single dollar bill, a quarter and two dimes in the corner of Brent's tray happened to catch Jevic's eye. That's it, he thought, as he grabbed the dollar from his buddy's tray.

"Can I borrow this?" he asked.

"Sure," Brent answered, before even knowing what he was referring to—that was just the kind of guy he was.

Jevic folded the bill right down the middle, opened it up and tore it in half. Brent looked at him like he'd lost his mind.

"What the hell?" he asked.

Jevic was so impressed with his idea that he didn't even

hear him. "Brent, I need you to do me a favor," he said with an unusually serious look on his face.

"If you only wanted half a dollar, I have another quarter in my pocket," Brent told him.

Jevic didn't laugh. He didn't even crack a smile, which immediately peaked Brent's full attention.

"Brent, I'm not joking around," Jevic said with an expression so serious that it didn't look like it could possibly be on the right face.

"Okay, Jev. What's up?" Brent asked.

"Take this. Hang on to it, and don't ever lose it. Ok?" he instructed. "I need to know that you are…" he stopped and thought about how to phrase this without sounding weird. "I can't explain, but I need you to keep that with you all of the time. All right?" he asked as he handed half of the bill to his friend.

"I'll have to hang on to it now; I can't spend it," Brent noted, shaking his head at his friend's irrational behavior.

"I might ask for it back sometime, so keep it with you just in case," Jevic added.

"Yeah, yeah," Brent patronized. "You sure you didn't fry your brain too?" he teased. He slipped his half of the bill into one of the empty plastic picture sleeves in his wallet, and as he returned the wallet to his back pocket, he said, "I'll keep it right there next to my heart."

Jevic wished he could tell him everything.

"You sure you're all right?" Brent asked him again.

"Yeah, why?" Jevic replied.

"You just don't seem like yourself lately."

"Must be something to do with these stupid burns," Jevic lied again.

"If there's something else bothering you, Jev, you know you can trust me, don't you?"

"I know," he answered–now that there's a way to tell it's really you, he thought.

Just then, the girls joined them at the table. They sat down and started chatting about some new haircut Christina's friend

Ashley had. Brent rolled his eyes. Jevic shook his head and leaned back in his chair.

Brent watched Jevic across the table. He didn't know why he was acting this way, but he hoped he'd ask for help if he needed it.

Jevic cradled his bandaged hand against his chest and thought, I just hope he never loses his half of that dollar, or I won't know who to trust.

12 ~ THE OLD ~

Jevic had to find out if the Knights Templar had any historical presence in upstate New York. While the small town where he lived had no mall or theater, it did have a really old library, which would be an excellent place to start looking for…well, he wasn't exactly sure what he was looking for. And he definitely couldn't ask people for help, but maybe he could find another clue in a book or something. Yes, it was a long shot, but that was all he could come up with.

He pulled up in front of the old brick building and stuffed his bike into the rack out front. When the green screen door squeaked open and slammed closed with a bang behind him, the dark-haired woman, with glasses balanced on the very end of her nose, shook her head disapprovingly from behind a desk the size of a pool table.

"Sorry," he breathed in less than a whisper.

Jevic would be the first to admit that this was one of those places he didn't often visit. In fact, the last time he'd been there was about a year ago, and that was to borrow a book on Ireland for Alicia. If necessary, he chose to use the school library or the computer lab, which was exactly what had gotten him into trouble the night before. Quite honestly, this is about the last place in the world that anybody who knew him would be looking for him.

Reference, Cooking, Gardening and Hobbies the sections were labeled. Nothing jumped out at him until he came to a wall where the shelves went all of the way up to the ten-foot ceiling. It was marked Local History and located in the back corner where the light was not the best. Judging by the dust on these books, the woman at the front desk wasn't paid to clean. Although it was still a mystery to him what he was looking for, he started with the shelf that was eye level and moved from left to right hoping his gut would lead him to something, the way it tried to lead him away from that kid Eric.

There seemed to be a lot more history to his small town than Jevic had been aware of. He came across one book filled with pictures of really old buildings, many had been taken back in the 1800's. One of the more famous buildings had been a mill down by the river that produced gun powder. It had accidentally blown up on more than one occasion, which happened to be one story Jevic did recall from social studies class.

Apparently Robert Reilly's ancestors originally owned half of the land the town was now built on. However, the town was named after the local Iroquois tribe that planted a Peace Tree with the settlers. There was a mansion where George Washington reportedly once spent the night. Jevic recognized this building as the one by the Hoosick River that was supposed to be haunted. The place had been falling apart, brick by brick, until the historical society stepped in to raise money for its restoration. Now they held regular pancake breakfasts and barbecues there to raise funds, which pretty much ruined its reputation as the most haunted house in town.

Before the first hour had passed, Jevic was making himself at home; sitting cross-legged on the floor with a stack of books beside him. He'd worked his way down to the lower shelves but hadn't found anything of great significance yet. Searching through the dusty archives had left the bandage on his hand looking more like a dirty dust rag. I wonder how much they'd pay me to give this whole place a once over, he thought. Was this just a waste of time? What time is it anyway? He'd left the house in such a hurry that morning, he'd forgotten his phone. So he slid the stack of books back onto the shelf and walked along the back wall looking for a clock. When he saw the rolling ladder in the far corner, he walked over and gave it a little tug. It worked. His eyes followed the ladder's track all the way back to the Local History section he'd been browsing.

Jevic put one foot on the bottom step and pushed off with the other. Who knew a library could be so much fun? The ladder rolled smoothly along the back wall. It didn't take as long as he'd have liked to reach the other side of the room. When the ladder came to rest, he climbed all of the way up and started browsing titles on the top shelf. These books had three times the dust on them as those on the bottom shelf. Jevic wondered if that meant they were three times as old or if the lovely lady up front disliked heights even more than noise.

A large black book with a red binding that was in particularly rough shape caught Jevic's eye because the title had completely worn off the spine. He turned his back to the ladder and leaned against it as he opened the cover. It was filled with old maps of the area. Everything looked so empty and different from how it was now. As he turned the pages, he realized it contained maps from the settlement period as well, and they were all dated. Now, this might be useful, he told himself, placing it back in its original spot but leaving it pulled out so he could find it more easily.

What was he was really looking for anyway? He hooked his thumb in his side pocket and let his burned hand rest for a while. The more he used it, the more it bothered him. He still hadn't had a chance to come up with a story to tell his parents. They'd probably be home by the time he got there. What time was it? He held the ladder with his right hand and leaned out around the corner of the shelf in front of him. There was a clock on the wall above the front door. It was four forty-five. His parents would be home by six o'clock.

As he started down the ladder, it began to move with him at the top of it. Jevic looked down, but there was no one there.

In fact, there was no one anywhere in sight. Maybe the old building wasn't level or the ladder had a bend in the track that had caused it to roll. But it kept going for about eight feet before it jerked to a sudden stop.

As he looked up to examine the track above his head, an icy chill passed right through him. No wonder I don't like these places, he told himself. It's creepy here. Once again, he started down the ladder, and without warning, a small book fell off of the highest shelf and hit him on top of the head. Instinctively, he reached out and caught it with his left hand. "Ouch," he hollered. The pain was excruciating.

"Shhh," the librarian hissed from the front of the building.

The shower of dust that had sifted down from the upper shelf made his nose itch, and his burned skin hurt when he wrinkled it up to fight off the inevitable sneeze. He wrapped his left arm around the ladder to hold on. "Ahh choo!" he blasted, and the ladder was rolling back toward where he'd started.

Certain that the place couldn't be leaning in two different directions at the same time, Jevic hung on as the wooden steps rolled faster and faster toward Local History. The book with the red binding was still hanging off of the shelf where he'd left it. When the ladder hit that book, it came to an abrupt standstill, exactly where the strange ride had begun.

All he wanted to do was get off of that ladder, but something held him back. Maybe it was his gut, maybe it was his head, but something was telling him that he was supposed to take that book of maps too. He grabbed it from the shelf and held both books against his chest with his bandaged hand as he climbed down.

When both feet were on the floor again, he further examined the ladder and gave it a little shove. Then he turned his inquisitive eyes on the smaller book in his hands. It had no title on the spine, but on the black leather cover were well worn golden letters that spelled "Journal." He flipped it open to find page after page of handwritten text with dates in the upper right corners.

This was it. His gut was telling him that this was what he'd come there for. His gut also told him it was hungry again. So he took the books up front to sign them out.

By the time Jevic got back home, his hand was really sore. He had been too busy to come up with an explanation for his parents. Burns were prone to infection, and he could just imagine his mother's reaction when she finally sees his hand. He was quite sure he'd be rushed off to Urgent Care, before dinner.

As he pulled into the long driveway, he got a glimpse of something running alongside the creek toward Apple Rock. He carefully leaned his bike against a tree, which smiled hospitably. Then he slipped his backpack off and laid it in the grass near the trunk.

As headed upstream, he saw it was again. It looked like Aaron's wood elf guise. If the prince was looking for him, he'd surely look at Apple Rock. So that's where Jevic headed.

The lovely tree smiled as he approached. "Hello!" she greeted as soon as she saw him, which was a bit of a surprise, until he remembered the blossom in his pocket.

"Hi," he called back. "Have you seen Aaron?"

"No, but he sent his page here with something for you."

At the base of the tree sat a piece of paper and a small round box that appeared to be made entirely of leaves. Intrigued with the little container, Jevic picked it up for a closer inspection. Various green leaves had been pasted together in layers and shaped into a perfectly round little box with a matching lid. He set it down carefully while he read the note that was with it.

Jevic,

I wanted to get you home safely last night and did not have time to give your hand the proper care. This ancient herbal medicine is very effective in healing burns like the ones you sustained. Apply the salve in this container to your wounds. I'm sure you will notice a difference.

I apologize for not coming to meet you myself, but my

father is not well. I fear his heart is running out of summers.

Be careful, and I will see you soon.

Yours in friendship,

Aaron

Jevic folded the letter in half and stuffed it into his pocket. Then he sat down on his branch and removed the filthy gauze from his hand. What a mess! Huge water blisters covered the entire top of his hand and all of his fingers. There were sections of skin burned so badly that it had turned brown, somewhat resembling fried chicken. When the air hit it, the pain was nearly unbearable.

"Alicia has told me stories about fairy medicine," he said. "I hope they are true."

He removed the fragile lid from the top of the box. Its creamy, white contents smelled like fresh flowers as he dipped his finger into the salve, but then he hesitated. What if this wasn't from Aaron? Could he trust that it was really his page who had left it?

He looked at the tree and asked, "How can I be sure this is really from Aaron?"

"The messenger seemed sincere and extremely anxious to return to the prince in case he was needed," she answered.

How bad was King Ronan? Jevic's heart went out to Aaron. He knew how it upset him to even think of Alicia's health deteriorating. If only he could do something to help. Suddenly, it occurred to the young Seer–helping was exactly what he was trying to do. And if what he'd been told was correct, he was the only one who could help.

Expecting it to hurt like the devil, he scooped up a gob of salve and applied it carefully to his wounds, but it didn't hurt. In fact, as he smoothed it over the blisters, the pain subsided. He scooped up another gob and worked it around all of his fingers and onto his face without a second thought.

Aaron is really looking out for me, he thought, remembering the way he showed up just when he needed him most. Jevic closed his eyes, thoroughly enjoying the benefits of the medicine for a moment before he slipped the cover back into place and slid the box into his pocket.

As he wadded the dirty bandages into a ball and shoved them into the back pocket, he told the tree, "I have to go eat dinner. See you soon."

Fortunately, his parents weren't home when he burst through the door and tossed his backpack on the floor. He hollered for Alicia, but there was no answer. He noticed her bedroom door was ajar and called her again as he pushed the door open. His grandmother was lying on the floor beside the bed.

Jevic ran to her side and dropped onto his knees. "Alicia!" he shouted desperately. He laid his hand on her back. She was breathing.

"Alicia, can you hear me? It's Jevic. Alicia?"

"Jev?" She answered so softly that he could barely hear her.

"Yes, I'm right here," he told her.

The old woman lifted her head and tried to push herself up.

"Are you sure you're not hurt?" he asked as he helped her onto the bed. "What happened?"

"I don't remember," she answered.

"I'll get you some water," Jevic said as ran to the sink. He was back in a few seconds. "Here take a drink," he urged, helping hold the glass.

She closed her eyes for a moment. "Thank you, dear. I'm much better now," she assured. A look of confusion seized the old woman's face, and she reached out to touch Jevic's hand.

"Your hand, your face!" she whispered. "What happened to your burns?"

Jevic looked at his left hand, which appeared perfectly normal. Then, wondering if it had been the other, he looked at his right. There was no sign of a burn anywhere. He looked over his shoulder at the mirror on Alicia's dresser. His face wasn't red either. He wrinkled up his nose and it felt normal. His expression was that of utter amazement when he turned back toward his grandmother.

"It's a miracle!" Alicia declared.

"It's fairy medicine. Aaron sent me some to put on my

burns," he told her as he reached into his pocket and produced the interesting container.

"What a lovely box," Alicia commented, but before she could touch it, the box vanished. "Good heavens!" she breathed.

Jevic raised a brow and stared down at his empty hands. Alicia grabbed hold of them again, turning them over for a thorough inspection.

"Thank God, you're okay," she whispered while collapsing back onto her pillow.

"But you're not," Jevic said. "What's wrong? Are you in pain? Do you want me to call a doctor?"

"No, I'll be fine," she answered. "I'm just not feeling well lately. I just need to rest a bit."

Jevic sat down on the bed beside her, and she reached up to touch his face. "Just amazing," she remarked again.

"You're not the only girl who thinks so," he joked.

Alicia smiled. "What wonderful medicine those people shared with ya, Jev. They must truly care about you."

"They do, Alicia. They are good people," he professed. Then suddenly, he had an amazing idea. If the Sidhe had medicine like that, and live so long themselves, maybe they had something that could help her.

13 ~ THE JOURNAL ~

When Jevic read the entire contents of the old black book that night, his instincts about the journal were confirmed. On the cover page was a small sketch of two knights on a single horse, the symbol of The Knights Templar. Many of the entries were related to the writer's personal affairs, which was a little creepy. But the guy who wrote the journal had been dead for about 200 years. So it's not like Jevic was really invading someone's privacy. Besides, there were a few passages the young Seer was absolutely certain fate intended just for him.

15th August, 1789

A storm delayed its arrival, but the ship safely ported in Albany this morning. The item we had been waiting to receive was on board in a sealed crate. There was much debate among the brothers as to where it would best be kept, and it was decided to temporarily house it in our Order's meeting place. It will be safe there until a more permanent location can be determined.

3rd September, 1789

Today the brothers agreed the safest place for this new addition to our trust would be a more remote location. This relic is coveted by many, and until rightful ownership can be determined among the many peoples who would have it, it is our duty to keep it secure. I and three others have been chosen to relocate the item tomorrow night.

4th September, 1789

Earlier tonight, we relocated that which has been entrusted to us. As we prepared to lift it from the wagon, however, the horses were spooked and we were unable to prevent the crate from falling to the ground. Unfortunately, the seal was broken. I managed a glimpse of the contents as we replaced the lid. If this is what I believe it may be, it is quite understandable why so many would have it. If it is indeed authentic, either the royal family does not know they possess a fake or they've ignored its lack of approval for the past five hundred years. Nevertheless, it is now hidden safely away where the earth will keep it from both the living and they who are not.

When he'd read the final entry, Jevic flopped back onto his bed with the journal open on his chest. Who had written these words? There was no name on the book. In fact, not a single name had been mentioned in the entire journal. If the knight this book had belonged to was as good at hiding the Stone as he was at concealing his own identity, this was not going to be easy.

If they could move it by horse and wagon in a single night, it has to be somewhere nearby. "It is now safely hidden away where the earth will keep it from both the living and they who are not." Jevic thought about those words. If the earth was keeping it, then it would have to be someplace wild, possibly with a natural barrier of sorts to protect it. The writer obviously knew the spirits from the Otherworld would also be looking for the Stone. But where could it be hidden that they couldn't reach? These were people who put on one impressive light show for him the other night. They had no problem reaching into the heavens. Where could they not go? Something about that line pulled at him. It had to be a clue. Somewhere in those words Jevic knew he'd find the direction he needed.

Direction, Jevic thought, as he set the journal aside and

opened the book of maps. The hand drawn maps were so old that at first it was difficult to relate them to the small town he had grown up in. The only way was by using the geographic features of the area. The Hoosick River was the local tributary to the Hudson. Although there was more rural housing now than farmland, and easily ten times the number of streets, the river was clearly the same on every map.

Some of the maps were drawn even before the railroad tracks had been laid along the river. Jevic's school wasn't on any of the pages. There was a school indicated on a back street in the village, although he was pretty sure one of the kids in his class lived in that building now.

Many of the oldest structures were no longer there, like the powder mill. William Reilly had apparently owned every piece of open land in town, and then some. From what he'd read about the Knights Templar, many of these men did not have a wife or family; and all had to take a strict vow of poverty. So he was pretty sure that whoever had written the journal was no ancestor of Robert Reilly's.

Jevic knew it was a long shot, but he scanned the pages for a place the Knights may have used for meetings. If he knew that location, it would give him some idea of where the Stone could have been moved that night. There was nothing obviously labeled "meeting house." There were a few churches and a grange hall, but then, they could have met in the woods, a member's home, or practically anywhere.

Jevic fell asleep thinking about that one haunting line in the final entry and woke up thinking about it the next morning. Still, he was no closer to understanding what those words meant. Like most people, he was usually happy on Friday, but school now seemed to be nothing more than an inconvenience every day of the week. He was just wasting time there. Maybe I should ditch school today, he thought. He'd probably get caught, and that fight in the cafeteria had already upset his father enough. He couldn't take a chance on getting into trouble again so soon.

The morning dragged, and Jevic couldn't think about

anything other than the last line in that journal. At lunch, it was still gnawing at him. What kind of place could the writer possibly be alluding to? Maybe it was a word puzzle instead of a riddle. He pulled a pen out of his pocket and wrote the line down on a paper napkin. Just as he'd finished, Heather sat down in the seat next to him.

"What's that?" she asked.

"Oh, nothing," Jevic lied.

"People don't usually write nothing down on lunch napkins," she said with a knowing smile.

Jevic grinned. "It's sort of a riddle I've been trying to solve."

"Want some help?" Heather offered. Her hair seemed curlier than usual today and hung down into her eyes like Jevic's often did. There was something about this girl that made him trust her. He was having no luck on his own and wondered if it would be so bad to take her up on the offer. There was no need to tell her anything, just see what she thought about the potential clue.

"Sure," he heard himself say before he'd had time to talk himself out of it. "Tell me what this means to you." Then he pushed the napkin over to the left side of his tray where she could read it.

"It is now safely hidden away where the earth will keep it from both the living and they who are not," she read quietly. Her eyes lifted as if she were looking at something floating in the air in front of her. "There aren't many natural obstacles that would protect something from both the living and the dead," she reasoned as she picked up her fork and knife to cut her salad.

"I know," Jevic agreed. "I've been driving myself crazy trying to figure out what it means."

Heather turned toward Jevic with a shy smile and stated one word quite confidently. "Water."

"Water?" he repeated in a doubtful tone.

"Living is living, and they who are not living are dead," she told him. "From what I've read, running water is the one obstacle spirits are unable to cross. It tends to slow most living creatures down as well."

"The river," Jevic murmured. Could it be in the river? His heart sank as he imagined the hopelessness of finding a rock like that in a river a couple hundred yards wide, which runs to some degree all year round.

Heather looked back at the napkin for a moment. "It wouldn't necessarily have to be in the river itself. The water could just be a barrier around the hiding place, like a moat around a castle."

Jevic recalled the maps he'd been studying the night before and pulled the old book out of his backpack. "Like an island?" he asked.

"Exactly," she replied casually.

He flipped the book open and jammed his finger enthusiastically into the page. "And there is an island!" he exclaimed.

Heather looked up from her plate. "That one is unofficially named Hippie Hill. A dozen hippies spent the rest of the summer camped out on that island after they attended Woodstock in 1969. No one knew who they were or where they were from, but they were very cool, according to my parents."

"How did they get out to it," Jevic asked.

"There's a dam that holds most of the water back during drier months so they can generate electricity with it. This time of year, you can make your way across the riverbed rocks and barely get your feet wet. I've been hiking there with my parents a few times," she told him.

"That sounds like fun. How do you get down there?" Jevic asked, knowing the island could be seen from the highway bridge that crossed about a hundred feet above the river.

"There's a path in back of the Presbyterian Church that leads you right down to the water," Heather informed him. "I can take you there and show you around the hill if you want."

Just then Brent and Christina set down their trays. "Take you where?" Brent asked.

"Hippie Hill," Heather said.

"Cool. I've always wanted to go down there," Brent told them.

"Why don't we all go," Christina suggested.

Jevic didn't know what to say. How could he look for the Stone if he had the three of them with him? "I...uhh...don't know," he struggled unsuccessfully to come up with an excuse.

"Come on, Jev," Brent urged, giving him a little nudge.

I can always go back alone once I know my way around, Jevic thought before he asked, "How about tomorrow morning?"

"Want to meet at the church parking lot at nine o'clock?" Heather asked, and without waiting for a single response, she added, "Be sure to wear sneakers or hiking boots, and bring a bottle of water. I'll make some granola bars for a little snack."

The four of them agreed on the time, and the table was buzzing about their plans. For a while, Jevic almost forgot the real reason he needed to go there. Then, a wave of panic swept through him. Was he about to drag his friends into the same danger he was tangled up in?

We're just a few friends taking a hike, he tried to reassure himself. Everything would be fine, wouldn't it?

It was a beautiful, sunny morning as the boys rode their bikes down Main Street and into the church lot where Heather and Christina were waiting for them. Christina lived just up the street, and Heather had her parents drop her off on their way to the Farmer's Market with organic produce they grew on their farm.

"Good morning," Christina shouted. Heather gave a little wave and smiled.

Jevic and Brent leaned their bikes against the guard rail that ran along the back of the parking lot. Then Jevic untied the hawthorn staff from his handlebars. He had told Brent he'd found it in the woods, and it was going to be his new hiking stick. That was believable enough. Besides, there was no way he'd take this trip without it.

They grabbed their water bottles and headed down a steep,

narrow path toward the river. Heather led the way; followed by Jevic, Christina, and Brent. When they reached the river bank, there were dragon flies and butterflies floating up and down the water's edge. The river was running, but nothing like it did in early spring. Jevic often watched it rolling and churning over the falls from his father's truck when they crossed the bridge. Nearly the entire riverbed was covered in rock now; huge, sprawling slabs of slate that had been cleaved and gouged out by the elements for centuries.

It was a bit of a challenge finding a path from rock to rock that would keep them moving in the right direction without stretching anyone's steps to the point they'd fall into the streams of water around them. Heather was obviously an experienced hiker and seemed to have no problem leading the others across to the small mountain-like island that rose up in the center of it all.

Jevic was impressed. He and Brent had been hiking with their dads for as long as he could remember, but he didn't know many girls who liked the sport.

When they reached the base of Hippie Hill, the four teens sat down for a drink. The island had several outcroppings of the same gray slate that made up the majority of the riverbed. Its lower half was covered with small shrub-like vegetation and there were taller deciduous trees on the upper half.

"That was fun," Christina said, "I'm glad you led the way, Heather. It would have taken me a long time to get here on my own."

"Yeah, you really know your way around down here," Brent added.

"My dad taught me to look as far ahead as possible and plan your route," Heather told them. "The base rock stays the same from year to year, but the river moves the smaller stuff around. So the trip is different every time I come here."

While the other three chatted, Jevic was looking the island over as best he could. Where could they have hidden that stone, he wondered? An outcropping of rock ruled out an entire section of the hill as a possibility. Below that wall of rock, a shale slide flowed all the way down to the water, leaving no place to hide anything. From what he could see, the rest of the hill rose up at a 45-degree angle with a single trail that climbed in a spiral to the top.

"Ready to hit the trail?" Heather asked.

"Sure!" Jevic answered. Christina and Brent nodded in agreement as they tucked their water bottles into their packs.

The trail was steep and apparently not very often traveled, evidenced by the tall grass and weeds they had to walk through. But there were plenty of tree roots crisscrossing the trail for footholds as they climbed. Jevic stayed alert, hopeful he might catch a glimpse of a large white stone hidden away in the bushes along the trail. Unfortunately, the only visible rocks were all dark gray.

Could he have been mistaken? Maybe the treasure that journal referenced wasn't the Stone after all. Nevertheless, Jevic had to admit it was a lot of fun being out with these three. They were joking and laughing all the way to the top of the hill where they found a nice sunny spot to rest and enjoy one of Heather's granola bars.

"These are great!" Jevic complimented.

"Yeah, are you sure you made them?" Brent teased.

"Brent! They are delicious, Heather," Christina said.

"Thanks. It's my mom's recipe, perfected when she was pregnant with me. That's about all she could eat for the whole nine months," Heather added.

"My mom ate deviled ham while she was expecting me," Brent said.

"That speaks volumes," Heather laughed.

"Yeah, yeah," Brent chuckled, turning red in the face when he realized how he'd set himself up for that one.

"So, Heather," Jevic asked, "Is there anything special about this place that you haven't shown us yet?"

"There's a cairn on the other side that we'll pass on our way back down," she answered.

"What's a cairn?" Christina asked.

"It's a pile of rocks stacked on top of each other," Jevic

told her. "Hikers use them to help mark trails so others can find their way. For centuries, they were built in European countries as monuments or landmarks. Alicia said there were hundreds in Ireland where she grew up."

"Wow, Jev," Heather said, "I'm impressed."

"I have a wealth of useless information," he told her.

"Where is it?" Brent asked.

"Down there," Heather said, pointing to the west. "I'll show you."

Christina jumped in line after Heather, followed by Brent, and Jevic hung back so he could check things out a little better. The trail spiraled downward at a steep pitch, reminding him of the descent under the dead oak. He took a deep breath and reassured himself that this trip was completely different. His friends were with him in the sunshine, and there was nothing horrible that could happen here.

One section of shoreline, which could be seen from above, was covered with driftwood; entire trees had washed up onto that side of the island. The water must be remarkably powerful here at times, Jevic thought.

He had fallen behind but could hear the others and hurried to catch up. They were standing around a wonderful cairn in a small clearing halfway down the hill. It was about two feet high and a foot in diameter. Whoever had built it had gone through a lot of trouble to find beautifully-colored rocks to contrast the gray slate that was so plentiful here. The cairn was composed of hundreds of rocks stacked with such painstaking perfection that the gaps between them were no thicker than a coin. His friends were admiring the intriguing monument as Jevic approached.

"Check this thing out, Jev," Brent shouted. "We should build one like it near the cabin."

"You guys have a cabin?" Christina asked.

"It's not finished yet, but we're working on it," Brent answered.

"You'll have to show us. Maybe we can all work on the cairn," Heather suggested.

"Sure, we could do that," Jevic answered as he walked closer. "This thing's awesome. I don't think we could compete with the guys who built this."

As he squatted down beside the rock structure to inspect its construction more closely, he felt his medallion under his shirt slide across his chest in the direction of the stacked stones. At first, he didn't pay much attention to it, believing it was moving along its chain by gravity alone. However, when he went to stand up, the medallion pulled so strongly toward the cairn that it lifted his shirt away from his body in a very obvious manner. Jevic slapped his hand quickly over the medallion and pressed it back against his chest. It was surprising how much pressure it took to hold it there. He tried to turn away and felt the chain twisting under his hand as if the medallion were trying to throw itself over his shoulder to reach the pile of stone now behind him.

What the heck's going on? He walked away while struggling to keep the medallion from exposing itself to his friends. Still, it continued to twist and turn in his hand, almost violently, in a fight to reach the cairn.

Brent noticed his friend's strange behavior and asked, "Jev, are you ok?"

"Yeah...a bee flew up inside of my shirt. I'm trying to get him out without getting stung."

Christina stepped away and squealed, "Oh, I hate bees."

Brent suggested, "Just pull your shirt off."

But that was the last thing Jevic was about to do. "No, I have him trapped. I'll just go over here and let him go so he doesn't bother anyone else."

Stop! He silently ordered the medallion. I get it. The cairn is important.

A hand unexpectedly rested on his back, and the medallion instantly dropped to his chest. "Did you get it?" asked Heather.

Hoping the strange struggle was over, he didn't move for a second or two. Then Jevic gave his shirt a little shake and answered, "Yeah, I got it."

"Good," Heather said with an enchanting smile. "Do you

want to get going then?"

Jevic nodded.

As he turned to follow the others down the path toward the river, he kept a safe distance from the cairn and one hand ready to control the medallion if need be. It was then that reality hit him and his heart beat faster with excitement. He'd just gotten what he came for.

14 ~ THE IMPOSTER ~

By 12:30 that afternoon, Jevic was back at home. Brent asked if he wanted to work on the cabin for a few hours, but he told him he had something else to do. It wasn't really a lie, but he still felt bad not being straight with him. What good would it do to tell him the truth anyway? Maybe he could help; more likely, he'd think Jevic had totally lost his mind. Anyway, if he was meant to know, he would, Jevic reasoned, which didn't ease his feeling overwhelmed and alone on this quest. He needed to talk to someone and decided to go to the Otherworld for a visit with Aaron.

Jevic was halfway to the triad when his hawthorn staff began to pulsate, bringing the young man to an immediate standstill. He instantly broke into a sweaty panic with flashes of events from the last time the staff behaved this way interfering with any reasonable thought inside of his head.

As he scanned the woods for movement, he wondered if making a run for the Triad would be his best bet. Since it was all uphill, the ten-minute walk would take him about five if he ran, two and a half if he was scared enough. His eyes combed over the familiar woods again and again as the vibration of the staff grew stronger.

At least it's daylight, he told himself; if I really want to see

127

what's coming. The yellow-toothed smile of King Magnus invaded his thoughts and a shiver ran down his spine. The staff shook again, but this time it didn't stop.

"There you are," he heard someone say, and he spun around to see Aaron about two steps away from him.

"Holy crap! You scared me," Jevic gasped.

Aaron laughed. "Still a bit jumpy from the other night, I see."

"You might say so," Jevic admitted with a smile. "I was just on my way to visit you."

He had opened his mouth to tell the prince everything that had happened when he realized the staff was still shaking violently in his hand. Jevic looked at Aaron standing in front of him, and he looked through the woods surrounding them. The spirit faces of the trees were casting a suspicious gaze on the man before him, confirming the uneasy feeling in the young Seer's gut. As the energy of the hawthorn staff surged through his arm in perfect time with his quickening heartbeat, Jevic could hear Aaron's voice inside of his head, "Trust your heart when your eyes deceive you."

"Did you have something important to tell me?" Aaron asked with a smile. "Have you found the Stone?"

The staff was now shaking as it had when he was standing before the Unseelie thrones. "No, I haven't gotten anywhere," he lied. "In fact, I can't find anything at all. I wanted to tell you that I'm sorry—I've failed."

Aaron shook his head with a look of disgust on his face. "I have to say, I'm very disappointed but not at all surprised."

It was then that Jevic knew this wasn't his friend. He would never discourage him. Aaron had always believed in him. Jevic held his persistent hawthorn protector with both hands across his thighs and struggled to hide its movement.

"My father will need that medallion back then," Aaron informed him.

Jevic looked him directly in the eye. Alicia had taught him that a person's eyes are the window to their soul. These eyes were familiar, but they weren't Aaron's. Instead, they bore distinct similarity with Eric's.

"I don't have it with me," Jevic told him.

The imposter gave him a skeptical glare.

"I forgot to put it on after my shower this morning. I'll run back and get it. Why don't we meet at the place I first found you?" Jevic slyly suggested.

A wave of panic flashed in the eyes of the man before him, and Jevic smiled.

"I don't know," the imposter replied.

"You don't know what?" Jevic asked.

"I don't know if I can meet you there," he answered.

"Do you have something more important to do than returning the medallion?" the young human questioned.

"Why can't you meet me back here?" the imposter asked.

"Call me sentimental," Jevic answered. "Surely you remember where that was, don't you?"

"Of course I remember," were the words that came out of the imposter's mouth, but the look in his eyes betrayed him.

"Then wait for me there. I won't be long," Jevic said with a toothy grin.

When the imposter did not move, Jevic's suspicions were confirmed. "You're not Aaron. Who are you?" he challenged.

The imposter made one last attempt at the deception, "What do you mean I'm not Aaron?" But the look in his eyes gave him away, and he knew it. He reached for the hilt of his sword and Jevic gave his hand a sharp strike with the end of his staff.

A chilling smile spread across the imposter's face and his appearance began to change. The prince's chiseled features transformed quickly to those of a pale-skinned boy with freckles. Aaron's long dark hair now blazed like a red flame, and the eyes that had given him away were locked on Jevic.

"Well, look who it is," Jevic mocked. For the first time in his life, he could feel his blood boiling in his veins. The opportunity to face the piece of crap that had set him up for that trip to hell the other night was something he'd been looking forward to. It was going to be a lot easier knocking the snot out of this guy than someone who looked exactly like Aaron. "You were right, Eric. Now things are about to get very interesting."

Eric no longer wore the leather armor and gold sword that belonged to the prince. Instead, he was dressed in a dark brown pair of pants and a matching vest with no shirt underneath. The scabbard that now hung at his side was much shorter, although it produced a wicked looking dagger when the Unseelie passed his hand over it.

There was no making light of this situation. Jevic had done nothing to offend this guy, yet there was no doubt in his mind that Eric intended to use that dagger. As he gripped the hawthorn staff tightly with both hands, its pulsing energy traveled up his arms and welled inside his chest.

Eric lunged, swinging the crescent-shaped dagger at Jevic, who deflected the attack with his staff. He then delivered a shot to the creep's ribs as the force of his missed strike threw him off balance.

"So the little boy has a big stick," Eric antagonized.

"Beats that potato peeler you're playing with," Jevic coolly returned fire in the verbal exchange, although quite surprised himself at how he handled the staff. "You thought you were really funny setting me up like that the other night, didn't you?"

Eric responded with a laugh that made Jevic's skin crawl. "Sorry I wasn't there to witness that for myself," he scoffed.

Jevic was so angry his hands began to shake. His fingertips dug into the hawthorn quarterstaff. "What have I done to offend you?" he shouted.

"You're still breathing," Eric sneered. "You humans think only of yourselves and leave nothing behind but your filthy stench upon wasteland."

"Like that gray hole you crawled out of?" Jevic argued. "You can't judge us all by the sins of a few."

"It's too late! The damage has already been done. Soon mankind will watch the world they took for granted wither around them," Eric threatened. "The Seelies are fools to believe there is good in any of you."

Eric then took another swing at Jevic, who was so distracted by his banter he narrowly managed to block it this time. However, he did manage to seize that after strike opportunity again and jerked the end of his staff upward, surprising his opponent with a blow to the jaw. Eric's head flew back and then forward again with that horrifying smile still engraved on his face.

"You wouldn't know good if it hit you upside the head just like that," Jevic provoked. Adrenaline had overpowered his fear, or maybe it was the energy of his staff that seemed to be flowing through his entire body now, but he was determined not to let this guy get the best of him again.

His Unseelie opponent lunged furiously at Jevic once more. This time he stepped aside, spun quickly on his heel and struck his attacker behind the legs with a powerful blow. Eric dropped to his knees but took only a fraction of a second to find his feet. And then, he was running toward Jevic slicing the air wildly with his blade.

Oh, God! I really ticked him off, Jevic thought. How could he get himself out of this? He really was not a fighter. He had no business pretending he was.

One swipe of the gleaming dagger caught the front of his shirt. The blade was so sharp it tore it wide open down the front, which exposed his gold medallion. Jevic was too horrified to look but ran his hand across his chest. He didn't feel any damage.

Shit! This jerk is really trying to kill me, he told himself.

Jevic tried to compose himself and focus. He had trained in Tae Kwon Do for a couple of years when he was younger. His dad had insisted he give it a shot, but he wasn't very good—that's why he quit. Oh, he could kick like a kangaroo, throw a punch that his opponents rarely saw coming, and do a better full split than anyone in the whole school. He just didn't like hitting people. Even if they were all padded up in protective gear, Jevic didn't want to hit anybody without a good reason. So he'd learned how to block very well, how to maintain his balance and how always keep his eye on his opponent during a fight. He'd also learned that if he did accidentally make contact with one of his punches it could shatter someone's nose, and he really didn't like that.

"Now look what you did," Jevic said with a smirk struggling to hide his growing sense of panic.

"I thought you left that home today," Eric growled.

"I lied," Jevic confessed with a shrug. "What do you want from a human?"

"I want you dead," the freckled boy replied.

"Why? What did I ever do to you?" Jevic asked.

"You are interfering with destiny," Eric spat his answer at the Seer.

"I'm just following my own destiny," Jevic argued.

"Not when I'm through with you," Eric shouted as he charged at him again.

Jevic planted his feet, the right one slightly behind him and turned outward with his left a half step in front and his knee bent. Rays of sunshine bounced off of the blade as the one wielding it cut large sweeping X's in the air between them. From high left to low right and high right to low left. Slice, slice, slice…WHACK! Jevic had waited for Eric to leave his abdomen wide open as he lifted his arm from low right straight up, and he'd landed a powerful strike across his diaphragm. He watched as his attacker folded in half at the waist and gasped for his next breath.

"We don't have to do this," Jevic suggested, feeling the slightest bit of remorse after the blow.

But when Eric straightened back up, the look of pure evil in his eyes erased hope of talking this out along with any sympathy Jevic had for him. This was no lunchroom fight. There was no principal here to stop the insanity before it got any uglier. This wacko was going to gut him like a fish if he didn't get the best of him first.

Before he was able to take another step, Jevic swung the hawthorn staff like a baseball bat and landed another solid blow, this time to Eric's left shoulder. He staggered sideways a step or two before he was moving straight at him again. Jevic stepped back. He had to maintain the space between them. If he couldn't reach him, he couldn't cut him. The Unseelie warrior kept closing that gap, and Jevic kept moving farther away, step for step, until Eric took two running steps and dove for him. Jevic's eyes were fixed on the blade as the guy with the red hair swung the weapon in the direction of his throat. He ducked to one side and hammered the arm holding the dagger just above the elbow. There was a loud crack and Eric cried out in pain, but Jevic's sympathetic side had been put in its place by his will to survive.

"I'm going to kill you for that," Eric threatened, switching the dagger to his other hand and stabbing repeatedly at him again with unbridled fury.

One strike after another, Jevic successfully blocked the blade with the hawthorn until Eric pulled his swing short and jabbed quickly from a different angle.

There was a sudden searing pain in Jevic's upper arm. He staggered backwards, dropping his staff as his left hand clamped onto his right bicep. The Unseelie's haunting laugh rang unmercifully in his ears as he watched the sleeve of his shirt turn bright red. His fingers were warm and wet. And with every beat of the drum inside his head, came another gush of life from his wound.

Eric stepped closer, the edge on his dagger proudly stained red. "Yes, now things do get interesting," he breathed in a discomforting whisper.

Jevic's mind scrambled to find a way out of this. He lifted his staff from the ground at his feet and tried to reason with his enemy. "Killing me won't make a difference."

"You underestimate yourself," Eric argued. "It will make more of a difference than you will ever live to know."

Jevic tried to ignore the intense pain long enough to think. He was bleeding badly and running out of time. He pounded his hawthorn staff on the ground like he'd done that night in the Unseelie palace. This time there was no burst of light, no laser-like beacon for help shooting from it. His vision blurred and the woods began to spin around him. He dropped his head to his chest and looked at the golden medallion against his skin. Then he lifted his eyes toward his enemy.

Eric sheathed his dagger and stepped closer. Jevic had all he could do just to stay standing. As the woods whirled around him, he watched Eric reach for his medallion.

His mind screamed, "No! You can't let him take it!" But his body could not respond.

As Eric's fingers made contact with the golden tree, there was a brilliant flash that hurled him through the air like a rag doll. He landed in a heap on the forest floor twenty feet away.

Jevic didn't know what had happened and didn't care. He struggled to regain control of his body. Holding his staff feebly in his right hand, he clasped his left over the wound as tightly as he could, and his feet stumbled along in the direction of home. The faces on the trees looked on encouragingly as Jevic fought to stay conscious long enough to make it back to the house. On his way up the slope from the West Brook and tripped over a root that took him down on one knee.

"God, just help me get home," he prayed, struggling to get back to his feet. The tree spirits were no longer visible. He tried desperately to focus, but nothing was clear anymore. The forest was spinning wildly around him, and Jevic collapsed to the ground.

The young Seer rolled onto his back and looked up through the leaves at the blue sky. He wondered if Eric was dead or if he'd be coming to finish him off. And then there was a face looking down at him. He blinked hard, trying to see who the face belonged to and fought to lift his staff from where it laid motionless across his chest.

"Jevic, it's Aaron," a voice echoed as if from a dream at the same time he felt a great deal of pressure around his left arm.

No, not again, Jevic thought. He couldn't fight any more. He couldn't move but somehow managed to ask that question again; the answer to which only the real prince would know. "Where did I first find you?" he breathed.

"In the ferns by Apple Rock," the prince answered without

hesitation.

"I knew you'd come," Jevic murmured as his right hand fell away from the staff.

"You'll be all right, Jevic. I will take care of you," Aaron vowed.

"Aaron—I think I found it," he whispered, as the prince's face faded into the darkness.

15 ~ THE IMPOSSIBLE ~

As a fragrant breeze moved the curls across Jevic's forehead, his heavy eyes slowly opened to an incredibly brilliant light. He'd melted into the bed beneath him, like butter on warm bread. His limbs felt anchored to the sheets, like every ounce of energy had been drained from them. When the gentle breeze made another pass, gauzy curtains rippled all around him.

Am I dead, he wondered? When he lifted his head from the silky pillow, the gold medallion glided along the chain that hung around his neck. He suddenly remembered what had happened and looked at his right arm. A pure white bandage covered it from elbow to shoulder, and he breathed a sigh of relief. I don't think they use bandages in heaven, he reassured himself.

Anxious footsteps moved across the floor as a shadowy figure approached, and the curtain tore open on the left side of his bed. Deeply worried, Prince Aaron smiled for the first time since he'd found the young man near death in the woods.

"You scared the hell out of me, out of all of us," he said, sitting down beside Jevic on the bed.

"Sorry," Jevic answered hoarsely as he struggled to pull himself into a sitting position. He looked around the room and grinned. "I think you scared me more–putting me in a fancy bed, like this. Thought I'd died and gone to heaven."

Relieved to know the young man still had his sense of humor, Aaron gave him a solid pat on the back. "This was my uncle's bed chamber," he told him. Then, shaking his head ever so slightly in disbelief, he added, "You have proven yourself again, Jevic."

"How?" Jevic asked. Blurry memories were swimming chaotically inside his head. He remembered the fight, pieces of it anyway. He thought he'd done a pretty good job defending himself, until he got cut. He remembered Eric reaching out to take his medallion, which triggered an unsettling thought, and he reluctantly asked, "I didn't kill that guy, did I? He probably deserved it, but I didn't really want to hurt anybody."

"No, Jevic, you didn't kill him. And you were only defending yourself," Aaron justified with a nod toward his bandaged arm. "That Unseelie's blade was laced with poison. You lost a lot of blood, which washed much of the poison from your wound, but it very nearly killed you anyway."

"How did you find me? My staff didn't work like it did the other night, and I didn't think you were coming," Jevic's voice cracked with emotional recollection.

"Your staff only flares like that here. In your world, the energy travels down into the earth. The tree spirits also alerted me that you were in danger. Even they were afraid for your life."

"Where's that guy now?" Jevic asked as his heart began to race. He didn't want to admit it, but he was understandably terrified of meeting up with him again.

"He's being held for trial," Aaron replied. "He will be punished for what he's done to you."

"Punished how?" Jevic asked.

"He will be stripped of his powers to Change and be confined to this realm. You shouldn't have to worry about ever running into him in your woods again," the prince reassured with an understanding smile.

"I was holding back," Jevic smirked, "You'll be doing him a

favor keeping him away from me." Then he slowly rubbed the gold medallion between his fingers and asked, "What did this thing do to him anyway? I thought this was just bling, but it really sent that jerk flying."

"It's meant to protect you, like your staff," Aaron explained. "The medallion has powerful energy of its own, but no human has ever worn it before. I honestly didn't know how it would act with you wearing it. Apparently it has the ability to channel your will, as it would if you were Sidhe."

Jevic raised an eyebrow and gave the mysterious charm an appreciative squeeze in the palm of his hand. Suddenly he remembered why he'd been looking for Aaron in the first place and exploded with excitement, "I almost forgot. I may have found the Stone!"

"You really did?" Aaron asked. "I thought you were delirious when you told me that."

"Yeah! I found a journal that pointed me in the direction of an island in the river, not too far from here. My friend, Heather, helped me figure that out." He paused briefly to clarify, "Don't worry, I'm not telling anyone anything." Then he continued, "So my friends and I went to the island where we found this awesome cairn, and my medallion kept pulling me toward it like a magnet."

Aaron had been listening to the young Seer's every word, but when he spoke of the medallion's attraction to the cairn, he was much more intense.

"Aaron, I think that pile of rocks will lead me to the Stone of Destiny," Jevic told him enthusiastically.

"You may be right," the prince agreed. "My father's own medallion has pointed him in the direction of his heart's desire on more than one occasion."

Although his news was definitely promising, Aaron was most amused by Jevic's zealous attitude and couldn't hold back a smile. A few short hours ago, this young man was fighting for his life, and now he was bursting with excitement. That was the human spirit the Seelies believed in.

"I'm so thankful your strength is returning," Aaron told

him. "And I'm very proud of everything you've done to help us, Jevic. However, I fear it may be too late. My father's strength is fading, and Magnus is preparing his army for an attack. When my father passes, the Unseelies will invade our kingdom like a plague."

"No!" Jevic shouted. "I can get the Stone before King Ronan…" He stopped himself, as if speaking of the king's death would cast a shadow of doubt. "I'm sure I can find it. Please, let me talk to your father."

Aaron was quietly struggling with the possibility of his father's passing and had begun to lose heart, until now. After everything he'd been through, there was this young warrior, looking at him with hope-filled eyes. Of course he would bring that Stone back in time.

"He's in and out of consciousness. I don't know if he will be able to hear you," Aaron explained, "But if you wish to speak with him, come with me."

Jevic threw the beautifully embroidered blanket that had been covering him aside, and realizing he had nothing on but his medallion and his boxers. He pulled it back quickly to cover himself. Aaron roared with laughter.

"What the hell? Where are my clothes?" he asked, as abundant color returned to what had been very pallid cheeks.

"They were washed and repaired," Aaron chuckled. "I couldn't send you home with blood soaked clothing, could I?" He walked to a chair in the corner and retrieved Jevic's clothes. "I'll wait outside while you dress," he chuckled.

As it turned out, the young man's spirit was much healthier than the rest of him. When he hopped out of bed, he was terribly dizzy and grabbed hold of the curtain to steady himself. After a few seconds, he slipped into his shorts, which had been impressively laundered and had all of his belongings back in the correct pockets. He couldn't even tell where his shirt had been mended as he slipped it over his head while stepping into his sneakers. His arm was not as sore as he'd expected it to be, but then he was already familiar with the power of Sidhe medicine.

Against the chair where his clothes had been, rested his hawthorn staff. As he wrapped his fingers around it, he realized just how thankful he was for the staff, and for the prince who had now saved his life for a second time. He could not help Aaron losing his father, but he wasn't going to let him lose his kingdom too.

On their way down the hall to the king's bed chamber, Aaron noticed Jevic was leaning heavily on his quarterstaff to keep his balance and stayed close.

"Are you sure you're feeling well enough to walk?" he asked.

"I'm just a little dizzy. I'll be fine," he answered, but the sweat beading up on his brow was a clear reminder of his vulnerable condition.

They entered King Ronan's bed chamber through a heavy oak door with gleaming brass hinges, and a guard closed it behind them. The light in the room was dimmer than the one Jevic had been in. A huge platform against the wall to their right supported the most marvelous bed he'd ever seen. Laying at the edge of a purple velvet field trimmed with golden was the kindly old king, who appeared to be sleeping peacefully as they climbed the steps of the platform.

Aaron, dropping down on one knee, touched the king's hand. "Father, you have a visitor. Jevic has come to see you."

Instantly, the king opened his sky blue eyes and nodded to his son with the faintest of smiles. The prince stepped aside, and Jevic knelt by the bed where the king could see him.

"I hear you were wounded," the king said.

"Yes, your Highness, but I'll be fine," Jevic told him. "I'm sorry you are not well."

King Ronan stared warmly at the boy and said, "I too will be fine. But each time I sleep, I travel closer to where the tree touches the heavens."

"That's why I wanted to speak with you," Jevic told him. "You have to hang on, just wait a little longer before you—go. I'm close to finding the Stone of Destiny. I only need another day or two. Please, Sire, don't give up on me yet," he begged as tear ran down his cheek, and he dropped his chin to his chest.

The Seelie King reached out and put his hand on the boy's head, "Give up on you?" he said, "Jevic O'Connor, you are the human spirit my people have always believed in, the light the Unseelies fear most. I will never give up on you."

Jevic lifted his head and looked into his old, blue eyes.

"You are an honor to my brother's name," Ronan told him. Then he looked at Aaron and asked, "How is his wound?"

"It's healing well, Father. We can probably remove the bandage before he leaves."

"Good," Ronan whispered. Then he reached out and touched the medallion against Jevic's chest. "It's time for you to finish this. When we next meet, I expect you will be carrying our sacred Stone home."

As he rose to his feet, the young Seer promised, "I won't come back without it!" And the king closed his eyes with a peaceful smile on his face.

"I've got to get going," he said, practically running past Aaron to the door.

"Wait. We need to be sure you're well enough. Let's have a look at that arm first," Aaron insisted.

"I can't let him down," Jevic argued.

The prince put his arm around the young man's shoulders and reassured him, "Refusing to try would have been the only way you could have let him down." Aaron paused briefly before adding, "Don't get yourself killed, Jevic. I can fight for my throne if it comes to that. Don't risk your life again."

It was hard to tell just how long it had taken for Jevic's wound to heal because of the difference in Otherworld time. All he knew was that when he'd gone looking for Aaron, it was lunchtime on Saturday, and he emerged from the opening beneath the oak around three o'clock that same afternoon. His arm had healed amazingly well with only a thin pink scar about six inches long where it had been cut clean to the bone.

As he stepped out from beneath the great oak, Jevic was greeted with warm welcomes by the Triad.

Oswin winked at the boy and said, "You've learned the

importance of knowing who your friends are."

Jevic answered, "Wish I was as good at knowing my enemies."

"And you've learned that staff is good for something other than a torch handle," teased Osmund.

"Yes," Jevic answered uncomfortably. "I can't thank you enough for this, Sir," he said appreciatively as he raised the quarterstaff toward the generous protector.

As the ground beneath the great oak moved back into place, Osred spoke, "You have done well, Jevic. However, those trying to stop you will not rest."

"I'll be back soon," Jevic said confidently as he walked away.

In a clearing near the West Brook he noticed a trail of fresh blood on the ground that made his stomach flip. At first, he thought someone had hit a deer with their car and it ran into the woods to die. Then he realized it was his blood, and it was everywhere. As he stood motionless in the middle of the clearing, visions of that fight just hours before flooded into his mind with vivid detail. He realized just how lucky he was–how close he'd come to losing his life.

Jevic turned in a complete circle, smiling broadly at the dozens of trees around him. "Thank you!" he shouted, "Thanks for saving me!"

In the distance, he could see the dead oak from the other night; its branches scorched from the Unseelie attack. There was no way he would let them destroy these trees too. Now it was his turn to save them, he told himself as he followed that trail of blood toward home.

16 ~ THE ISLAND ~

Time passed so differently in the spirit realm, and that had Jevic worried. His arm had healed completely, he'd nearly recovered from the poison in his wound, and his clothes were repaired, cleaned, and dried. All of that must have taken hours, more likely days. Yet his blood was still wet on the ground when he returned. Although the strange time difference between realms had worked to his advantage during recovery, it would likely have the exact opposite effect on his race to return the Stone.

In fact, his concern was justified. Magnus had troops of dark soldiers gathering along the great barrier that separated the Sidhe kingdoms. A dense forest of thorn trees, planted as a reminder that despite their differences there were some things all Sidhe had in common, like their love for the hawthorn. Unfortunately, the Unseelie's determination to take control of the Otherworld far outweighed everything else. The battle that was now brewing could be devastating to the Seelies. The only chance to prevent the imminent attack was to have a new leader named to the throne before King Ronan passed.

Jevic burst through the door of the stone house, leaned the quarterstaff against the wall and grabbed a Granny Smith apple from the bowl on the table.

"Alicia," he called out.

"In here, Jev," she answered from her bedroom.

She was lying in bed when he entered her room. "Are you feeling any better?" Jevic asked as he sat down beside her.

"Much better knowing you're all right," she smiled.

How Jevic wanted to tell her what had happened. He wanted to tell her about the imposter, the battle, and the scar on his arm, which he hoped would not fade completely. He wanted to tell her how very close he was to making a difference to the whole world so she could be proud of him. Instead, he just told her that he loved her and kissed her good-bye.

"Can I get you anything before I go?" he asked.

"No thanks, Jev. I'm fine," Alicia answered softly.

"I'm spending the night at Brent's house," he lied, "I'll see you sometime tomorrow. Okay?"

"Wait," the old woman said.

He stopped short, hoping she wasn't about to question his honesty.

"Promise to take good care of my boy," she asked of him.

"Don't you think Dad's big enough to take care of himself?" Jevic answered with a smirk. Then he walked back to the bed and gave her a hug.

"Don't worry. I'll be careful," he whispered into her ear. After another quick peck on her cheek, he took a big bite out of the green apple in his hand and mumbled, "I love my grannies most of all."

There hadn't been much time to devise a plan, but he knew he wasn't going to wait till morning to check out that island again. What are best friends for, he told himself as he picked up the phone. Brent answered at his house.

"Hi, Brent!"

"Hey, Jev, what's up?"

"I need to ask a huge favor," Jevic told him.

"Sure, what do you need?" he replied.

Jevic hated to lie and couldn't believe he was about to ask his friend to. "Can you cover for me tonight? I have something important to do, and I'm telling my parents that I'm sleeping at your house."

There was silence on the other end of the phone for a minute. "What kind of something important? You're not in trouble are you, Jev," Brent asked in a deeply concerned tone.

"No, nothing like that," Jevic assured him. "I just…have something to do."

There was another awkward silence before Brent said, "You're going back to that island, aren't you?"

"What gave you that idea?" Jevic replied uncomfortably.

"Don't forget who you're talking to. You've been acting weird for the past week, and you were hiding something from us by that cairn."

"Hiding something?" Jevic repeated, trying to make the idea sound ridiculous.

Brent was concerned, but even more annoyed at Jevic's unusual lack of honesty. "Come on Jev! A bee up your shirt? You and I both know if there was a bee up your shirt, you'd have torn that thing off in a heartbeat. Instead, you casually walk away to save everyone else from being stung. You're terrified of bees! Who the hell do you think you're kidding?"

Jevic was speechless. Brent is right, he thought. I am terrified of bees. He's seen me, more than once rip my clothes off to avoid a sting.

"I am going back there, but I'm not in trouble," he admitted.

"I'm going with you," Brent insisted.

"You can't. This is something I need to do by myself," Jevic told him.

"I'll just tell my folks that I'm sleeping with you in the cabin tonight," Brent argued.

"No," Jevic replied. "Thanks anyway, but this is something I have to do alone."

"All right," Brent reluctantly agreed. He seemed distant and quite put out as he added, "If you change your mind, give me a call. Don't worry, I'll cover for you."

"Thanks, Brent. I'll talk to you tomorrow."

"Be careful down there," Brent warned.

"I will," Jevic promised.

With his alibi arranged, he wrote a note to his parents and left it by the fruit bowl. After stuffing a few apples into his backpack along with a bottle of water, a flashlight and an extra granola bar that Heather had given him, Jevic pedaled toward town with his hawthorn staff tied across the handlebars. The ten-minute ride gave him plenty of time to second guess himself and feel bad about lying to the people he loved. But this was the only way to find that Stone and get it back to the Otherworld in time. He'd start looking at the cairn, but he honestly had no idea how he'd move the Stone once he found it. If it took four men to get it there, he was going to have to use his head to get it back alone.

After stashing his bike in the bushes behind the guard rail at the parking lot, Jevic hit the trail leading down to the river. Everything seemed to be going smoothly, and then it started to rain. By the time he reached the riverbank, the sky had really opened up. Jevic took his sweatshirt out of his backpack, pulled it on and threw the pack back over his shoulder as he headed across the wet rocks. Although the rain was blocking most of it, there were a few hours of daylight left. It was enough for him to find his way across the river stones to the island, despite the driving rain. His hawthorn staff once again proved useful, helping maintain his balance when stretching his steps a little further than he should have on the slippery rocks. Nevertheless, by the time he reached the trailhead on the island, Jevic was soaked. It was a miserable climb up that hill in the relentless rain. The path was muddy and the wind was picking up, but he didn't stop until he'd reached the top.

He didn't want to admit it, not even to himself, but Jevic was still weakened by the poison that lingered in his system. A growling stomach reminded him he had not eaten much in the last day. Considering what his body had been through, he knew it was best to take a quick break and maybe a snack. There was a willow tree nearby that would provide some shelter from the storm for a few minutes rest.

The young Seer smiled politely as he ducked beneath the willow's drooping branches and sat down on a piece of semi-dry ground at her feet.

The face of this tree was not as obvious as those in his woods, but he eventually made out an older female's features looking back at him from the water-soaked trunk. He assumed it was rain that had darkened the trunk. Until he realized the old tree was crying.

Jevic reached out with his foot to touch the root next to him. "Hi. My name is Jevic," he said.

"Are you here all alone in this horrible weather?" the willow sobbed.

"Yes," he answered.

"How terribly sad," she wept.

"Why are you crying?" he asked.

"Oooh, that's what I do when it rains," she wailed. "When the sun shines and the wind blows through my branches, I'm happy. But when it rains, I just feel like weeping."

"Do you mind my sitting with you for a while?" he asked.

"Noooo, I would enjoy some company," the tree cried. "It's nice to meet you. I'm Willowwwww," she replied.

Jevic tried not to laugh. "Willow, do you know anything about a special stone that may be hidden here on this island?"

"There are stones everywhere. Water everywhere, even falling from the sky."

"The stone I'm looking for is a special stone. Four men brought it here a long time ago to keep it safe," he explained.

"My mother told me a story when I was just a sprout," Willow sobbed, "Oh, mother, how I miss her."

"Was the story about a stone?" Jevic asked tenderly.

"Yes. Mother said the whole island grew up around one stone to hide it from those who would use it for bad things."

"I know those people," he said.

"How does a nice boy like you know bad people?" Willow wailed.

"They are trying to stop me from returning the Stone to the good people it belongs to," he explained.

"I knew you were a good boy," the tree whispered with a sniff.

Jevic asked softly, "Willow, will you tell me your mother's story?"

"I don't know if I remember it all."

"Just tell me what you do remember," he urged.

The tree was quiet for a moment before she started to share that story. "It happened a long time ago, before my mother had even sprouted."

Normally, Jevic would not have been able to keep from laughing at this bizarre conversation, but he was hanging on every word Willow breathed.

"Four men came in a boat with a rock wrapped in pieces of dead...wood," Willow stopped to sniffle again. Jevic sat up a little straighter on the ground near her feet. "They hid their stone under a pile of tiny rocks where no one could find it."

It is the cairn, Jevic thought. "Thank you, Willow. You've been a great help. I'll stop back to visit again when the sun is shining," he promised as he hopped onto his feet.

"I enjoyed your company...while it lasted," the tree cried.

Jevic tossed his backpack over his shoulder, picked up his staff and ran down the trail in the direction of the cairn. The rain, now coming down in buckets, was flowing swiftly down the hillside, especially along the trail, which was the easiest course for runoff. But it caused the usually sure-footed teen to slip and slide all the way to the small clearing where he came to a sloppy stop in mud up to his ankles. Before getting too close, he pulled the medallion outside of his sweatshirt where he could see it clearly. Instantly, it began to move. A steady stream of water ran down his face and into his eyes as the Tree of Life lifted itself into the air in the direction of the cairn. To his surprise, it guided him right past the structure, nearer the edge of the hillside, where it began to pull straight downward. Jevic stepped back. He moved to one side and then the other. However, no matter where he stood, the medallion always led him to the very same spot, three feet from the cairn.

A smarter guy would have thought to bring a shovel, he

told himself, giving the ground beneath his feet a few kicks. Huge drops of rain punched little holes in the water's surface above his submerged sneakers, but there was one hole that was different from the rest. It was a small whirlpool near the center of the puddle. There, the muddy water appeared to be flowing down into the ground rather than running off the steep terrain like everywhere else.

As Jevic squatted down to get a closer look, the medallion pulled toward that tiny whirlpool with such force its chain was digging into his neck. He jabbed the hawthorn branch into the mud, attempting to pry himself away from the ground. Instead, the ground pulled away from him, and without warning the earth dropped out from under his feet.

Although, the free fall lasted only a second or two, it stopped abruptly when his ass landed on a huge pile of mud. A shower of cold muck continued to rain down on top of him for several seconds after. Jevic couldn't open his eyes and struggled to breathe through the heavy coating of mud that completely covered him. One limb at a time, he escaped the mess and crawled blindly into a hollow area away from the lingering shower from above. An attempt to wipe his face with his gritty sleeve was useless. So he felt his way around and managed to pull a water bottle out of his pack, tipped his head back and poured it over his face to wash the dirt from his eyes.

The darkness around him was as heavy and cold as the layer of mud he was wearing. So he felt his way through the pack again in search of his flashlight. Finally, there was a click, but the beam traveled only a few feet before hitting a wall of dirt. Jevic moved the light from left to right and could see he'd fallen into a small hollow in the ground. In the center of the space was the great mound of mud he'd just crawled out of.

The beam climbed to the opening in the ground overhead, illuminating sparkling drops of rain as they fell through it from the dark sky. I should be able to pull myself out, he thought.

The light dropped back inside, finding the brittle roots of some long dead tree; for there was no sign of a stump on the surface. Yet as that beam swept through the small cavern, those roots appeared to be moving. From the dark earth, roots began to emerge, twisting and slithering like dozens of snakes. When those roots started closing around him like a living cage, he stopped questioning his eyes and started to question his reasons for coming here in the first place. Jevic flashed his light toward the opening overhead. From all directions, the roots were quickly weaving a barrier between him and the sky.

The moment he dared to think things couldn't get any stranger, a hissing noise from the darkness to his right demanded his full attention. The flashlight jerked in that direction and locked on a snake's head that was the size of a football and less than an arm's length away.

"Holy shit!" he called out as he scrambled in the opposite direction, completely forgetting about the wriggling roots until one tightened around his leg. He pulled his hawthorn staff from the mud beside him, and swung it at the serpent's head. It passed through as if it was made of air, and the head followed him. Jevic looked frantically at the opening above, which was rapidly growing smaller.

As if the snake could read his thoughts, it hissed, "Get out while you can."

Jevic took a second swing at the giant head. Again, it had no effect.

"You have no business here, human," it hissed. "Go back where you belong and meddle no more in things that do not concern you."

"This does concern me," Jevic heard himself respond without due consideration.

"Leave Sidhe concerns to the Sidhe. Heed my warning boy, for there will be no turning back from a poor decision." The serpent's voice sounded remarkably similar to that of the Unseelie King. "Get out before it's too late," the head threatened.

Jevic's eyes flashed from the snake to the mesh of roots forming around his only escape. As he tried desperately to peel a coiled root from around his hawthorn staff, another wrapped quickly, firmly around his neck. Using both hands, he jerked enough slack to slip his head free and immediately resumed the fight for his staff.

"You're running out of time. Interfere in our world and we'll interfere in yours," the snake warned quite convincingly.

"What the hell does that mean?" Jevic demanded, his teeth gritted with determination as he tore another root from his trusted hawthorn branch.

"Even those you hold dear are not beyond our reach. Go back to where you belong while you still can."

For a moment, Jevic seriously considered scrambling up the mound of earth in front of him and squeezing through the only space that was still big enough. Instead, he took a deep breath and listened to the calm voice of reason ever present inside his head. Why hadn't this thing taken the Stone for itself? If spirits can't cross running water, this thing can't retrieve the treasure any more than Aaron could. He had to be the one to take the Stone out of this place for them, and the Unseelies would rather lose it forever than have Aaron get it back.

"You're afraid of me," he challenged his captor, sounding much calmer than he felt inside.

The snake raised itself up as if about to strike back for his verbal attack. But Jevic, for some reason beyond his own comprehension, refused to back down.

"You're afraid of me, and you should be," he said defiantly to the head that was now inches from his face. "It's my destiny to return that Stone to the Seelies, and you know it."

The serpent flicked its tongue so close to the boy that he thought he felt the tip of it touch his nose, but he barely flinched.

"I'm not leaving this island without that stone, and I'm bringing it to the Seelie palace."

Several roots tightened suddenly, violently around him. One bound his right arm to the wall behind him, another held his left leg and one was so tight around his chest he could barely breathe. Jevic kicked at the root around his ankle with his other heel until he could slip his leg free. Then he loosened the tendril across his chest enough to work his staff under it. With a quick wrench upward, the root snapped. That technique worked so well that he repeated it to free his right arm. Whipping the staff wildly, he beat oncoming roots as they moved in his direction. Pieces snapped off, flew through the air, and lay writhing in the mud all around him.

"Fool," the serpent hissed, "You don't know what you're doing."

"I know exactly what I'm doing," Jevic shouted. "And I'm not leaving here without the Stone."

The snake unhinged its jaws, bared a terrifying set of fangs and lunged. Jevic threw himself clear, landing in the total darkness of the hollow with a blunt edge against the middle of his back. Instantly, the viper vanished, and the roots around him became as shriveled and lifeless as they'd been before. Jevic flashed the light around in disbelief. Then he turned it on the partially buried object he'd fallen against.

The beam bobbed up and down as Jevic held the flashlight in his mouth and used both hands to move some of the dirt away. He swept his forearm across the top of it and directed the beam onto the surface of a large white rock. An ornately carved Celtic border flowed across the side that faced him. On top, the Tree of Life was clearly visible; its recesses filled with mud in contrast to the white stone that proudly bore the symbol that was so sacred to the Seelies.

"Thank you!" he whispered lifting the mud-coated medallion to his lips. Jevic pressed his hand against the cold marble to be sure it was real. He ran his fingers along the beautiful knot that wrapped so perfectly around all four sides.

"I found it, Aaron!" he shouted. "Tell your dad, I'm bringing it home."

17 ~ MOVING MOUNTAINS ~

Jevic was filled with mixed emotions. It was truly unbelievable that he'd found what he'd come for. But how would he ever get this big block of marble out of its hole and back across the river?

The Stone was about ten inches high and 18 inches square. Jevic continued to clear away the dirt that had settled around the treasured relic over the centuries. When it was completely uncovered, the Stone looked exactly like the one King Ronan had projected; except quite a bit dirtier.

Maybe it was the fall of darkness. Maybe it was the fear of the next serpent's head or whatever test he'd have to face. Maybe it was that he'd nearly died a day ago and hadn't had enough time to recover before racing out into the cold night rain. Most likely, it was a combination of everything that finally took a toll on Jevic. He suddenly felt very much alone and terribly vulnerable.

What if the Unseelies followed me here? There have to be more creeps like Eric that they could send after me. His eyes left the Stone and focused on the gaping hole overhead. If they're on this island, they can easily find me and the Stone, he thought.

It didn't take long for the panic inside the young Seer to

grow like a snowball rolling downhill. What do I do now? What if the rain doesn't stop and the hollow fills up with water? What if more of the roof falls in on me? How will I ever get this thing out of here by myself?

He traced his fingers over the tree carved into the top of the marble. It seemed to have an almost hypnotic effect on him. He'd had a very long day, but he suddenly found it impossible to keep his eyes open. There was no fighting it. Jevic folded his arms on top of his treasure, rested his head on them, and decided to close his eyes for a minute...or two.

The water was so cold, but he had to keep swimming. Was he heading in the right direction? There was no sign of land anywhere. He was exhausted, and he just wanted to feel his feet on solid ground again.

A sudden jerk on his leg brought Jevic to a dead stop in the water. He pulled against it, but something had a hold on him. He took a deep breath and ducked below the surface to see what it was. There was a rope tied around his ankle. The knot securing it was tight, too tight to loosen. So he followed the rope deeper into the water where the other end was tied to a large white rock resting on the bottom. He tried desperately to move the Stone, but it wouldn't budge. His lungs were screaming for air. So he raced back to the surface for a breath.

But the water must have risen, for now he could barely reach the surface. He gulped only one more breath before going under again, and his desperate struggle to get his head above water for a second was useless. The surface seemed to be moving farther away. Or was he being pulled downward?

As Jevic fought to loosen the knot by his ankle, a red-haired boy with a disturbing smile swam up beside him. He held out a knife to Jevic, whose lungs were on fire.

"Take it–save yourself," the red-haired boy's words echoed inside Jevic's head.

"No," he thought. "You'll take the Stone when I go up for air."

"Will you really die for it?" Eric asked.

"Before I let you have it, I will," Jevic answered without any hesitation.

"Would you let Alicia die for it?" the Unseelie challenged.

"What do you mean?"

The sinister smile on his enemy's face sent a chill down Jevic's spine. "If she drinks this, she may live for many more years. Without it, this will be her last," Eric taunted.

"No," Jevic protested. "This can't be her last summer."

"Cut yourself free and bring this to your dear granny," Eric coaxed him.

Jevic looked down at the Stone and then up toward the surface, now far beyond his reach. His lungs were going to explode. The urge to inhale was unbearable as the red haired boy held the bottle and the knife out enticingly."

Jevic woke up screaming, "No!" and gasping for air. His head bumped against a tree root, raining a shower of dirt down upon him in the darkness. He was disoriented and panicked. Where is the light? Where am I? He needed to escape the overwhelming darkness that surrounded him. Fists and feet shredded the brittle roots blocking his way to the opening above. And not until he'd climbed up out of the hole did he realize it had all been a dream.

Jevic lifted his face toward the sky and took slow, deep breaths as the rain washed over him and his panic subsided. When he returned to the hollow, there were pieces of broken root everywhere. Too bad I didn't go the other way. I probably could have dug right through the side of this hill.

A Cheshire Cat grin spread across Jevic's face. Maybe that's how the knights got it here in the first place. I'll dig through the side of the hill. He felt around for the flashlight and turned its beam on the marble block. If they'd dug a hole and buried it, there would have been dirt packed solidly around it, which wasn't the case. There must have been a small cavern here originally. They slipped it inside and sealed it shut. If that was how they got it in here, then it was probably the best way for him to get it out.

Jevic poked at the wall of dirt behind the Stone with his staff. As he stabbed and scraped at the inside of the hollow, the dream he'd just had haunted his thoughts. What if Eric really did come after the Stone? Aaron would never let him leave their realm, not after what happened the other day. Besides, if what Heather had told him was true, Eric couldn't cross running water. Actually, the question that was really eating away at the young Seer was, could there be any truth to what Eric had said about Alicia? Her health had been failing.

It was just a stupid dream. How often do my dreams make any sense, Jevic asked himself as he continued to dig? Who wouldn't have a freaky dream after falling asleep in this place? Just yesterday someone tried to kill me. I'm tired and paranoid. I need to stop letting my imagination wander and get this Stone back to the Otherworld.

Suddenly the end of his staff passed beyond the point of solid ground. Jevic grabbed the flashlight and crawled on his belly to the spot where the hawthorn had disappeared though the wall. He slowly pulled it out, leaving a fairly clean opening behind. There was definitely air moving through it. Wedging the flashlight against the hole, he pulled himself out of the hollow and stepped cautiously toward the slippery edge. A few feet down the hillside from where he stood a fine beam of light was illuminating raindrops as they fell.

"I was right!" he shouted excitedly. Then, after taking a quick look around to be sure nobody was watching, he jumped back into the cavern.

I can widen that opening up before morning. There's no way I'm going to fall back to sleep again; one nightmare was more than enough.

Before there was even a hint of daylight, he'd finished, and he sat down to eat a granola bar while planning his next move. The hillside was so steep that it would be fairly easy to drag the Stone down the slope once he had it outside. However, getting it out through the side of the hill was going to take some work. As he finished what was left of his water and went to put the bottle into his pack, a thought occurred to him.

If I tie these straps together, it might be long enough to use as a harness. In a matter of minutes, the nylon straps were off of the bag and buckled together. He wrapped them around the Stone and set the ends near the opening where he could reach them from outside.

Jevic climbed out of the hollow and carefully down the slippery hillside to grab the straps. He pulled as hard as he could, but it didn't move. He planted his feet and tried again, and again. But no matter how he tried, it was impossible to stop from slipping on the sloppy combination of grass and mud covering the slope. Nothing could stay put in this slimy mess.

Alicia's voice whispered in his memory, "When life buries you in lemons, make lemonade."

Jevic dug the bottom of the exit hole a little deeper and scooped up a few handfuls of the slimy mud and grass combination he was standing in to coat the lower part of that opening. Then he scrambled back up the slope and down into the hollow.

With his feet braced against the wall of dirt behind him, Jevic pushed at the back side of the Stone. His legs wobbled and his arms shook with exhaustion, but he kept pushing. It had to move! He had to move it, and he was not going to let up until he did. He put his head down and his back into it until the marble slowly slid from the spot it had settled comfortably into over the ages. It was only an inch or two, but it definitely shifted enough so he felt his legs had room to straighten a little more in the cramped space.

It wasn't hopeless. He took a huge breath and pushed again. The Stone moved forward a couple inches more.

"Yeah, baby!" Jevic groaned through clenched teeth, "Keeeep moving." And it did. He readjusted himself, so his back was against the marble block and braced his legs against the dirt wall.

"Mooove!" he groaned while focusing every ounce of energy he could muster.

It was a painfully slow process, but it continued to gradually creep forward. Finally, when most of it was lying on the slimy layer of mud, it glided along with hardly any resistance at all until the back side of the Stone was flush with the inner wall of the hollow.

Jevic readjusted the strap so he could pull from outside and rushed back to the surface.

The rain had all but stopped now, and the piece of marble protruding from the hillside was tinted pink by the early morning glow on the horizon. Jevic grabbed the nylon straps from either side of the Stone, dug his heels into the hillside, and dragged the Stone of Destiny out into the open air for the first time in over two hundred years. With a little more effort, he hauled the sacred Sidhe treasure onto the wet slope as the first rays of sunshine broke through the trees near the steeple of the Presbyterian Church.

Jevic was out of breath and out of energy as he sat down beside the great Stone to take a good look at it. He brushed off the top so he could see the tree more clearly. Even with all the dirt, it was still one of the most wonderful things he'd ever seen. The power it possessed was undeniable, as it seemed to radiate a strange field of positive energy that was impossible to ignore but just as impossible to explain. The beauty and detail of its carvings were magnificent. Every cut was still so crisp and clear. As Jevic traced his fingers over them, the reality of what he'd accomplished sunk in.

Sure, he'd found the Stone. Great! He'd gotten it out onto the slope alright. But his challenges were far from over and he was totally exhausted. Maybe if he just rested for a few minutes, he'd regain some of his strength. As his body took a time out, his mind was busy wondering how he would ever get that block of marble off of the island.

Before could really begin to consider his options, a strange whistle sounded. Actually, it was more like a horn than a whistle that trumpeted through the river valley. It was a creepy sound he didn't recall ever hearing before now. Not at all as loud as the firehouse siren that went off when the volunteers were summoned into service, and every day at noon. That one Jevic could hear miles away at his house. This was a softer horn that traveled down the river from the direction of the dam.

Not a minute later, Jevic could see water spilling over the dam and a line of white moving over the rocks in his direction. It couldn't be…but in fact it was. The horn was a warning that they were opening the flood gates after all of the rain. It was intended to alert anyone who might be on the riverbed before the water began to rise, which is exactly what was happening.

The water that had been freed from the dam rolled toward the island like a bubbling white carpet. Jevic watched helplessly as it splashed into the rocks at the base of the island and rushed swiftly to either side in a race to the 50-foot fall that waited down river, not far at all beyond Hippie Hill.

He stood beside the Stone with his mouth gaping open in disbelief. What more could happen? He'd been burned, cut, had the skies open up on him, the ground drop out from under him, and now the river was cutting him off from the rest of the world.

"What the hell? I'm just trying to do the right thing here. Can't I get a break?" Jevic pulled his filthy sweatshirt off and threw it onto the ground. He kicked it, picked it up, threw it again and gave it one last kick for good measure. Then he threw himself onto the ground and dropped his head into his hands. Why did this have to be so hard? How would he ever get back now? He was stranded…stranded on the side of Hippie Hill like a battered piece of driftwood.

And that idea lifted the boy to his feet. "Lemonade!" he whispered. He picked up his sweatshirt and ran toward the shoreline where dozens of dead trees had washed up. He would build a raft and float the Stone back.

18 ~ WHAT FRIENDS ARE FOR ~

The early morning sunshine glazed the island with its magic, capturing rainbows in every drop that still clung to the scrubby bushes on the soggy hillside. But Jevic took no time to appreciate the beauty that surrounded him, the sheer wonder of this island that belonged to him alone, albeit only for a time. Had the situation been different, he may have reveled in the splendor of this opportunity. After all, what young man hasn't dreamt of having an island of his own? But the young Seer was not thinking about enjoying himself. This was not about him. All he could think of was the completion of his quest.

When Jevic reached the drift pile, an eerie feeling came over him. The whole side of the island was littered with lifeless limbs and trunks of trees that had once held beautiful spirits. The pile was huge. Where had they all come from? Where did the spirits go when the trees died? Did all spirits travel along the same Tree of Life? If so, then death was not the end but a new beginning in every spirit's journey. Finally, he understood what Alicia had been trying to tell him that day by the creek.

Jevic explored the pile of debris, searching for both logs and something he might be able to tie them together with. Trash and even a dead carcass of some kind had also washed up nearby, making his scavenger hunt rather unpleasant.

Along the shoreline, he found one tangled strand of nylon fishing line after another, which he gathered up and stuffed into his pocket. His most exciting discovery was an entire wooden pallet that would make a perfect platform for his raft. Jevic dragged the pallet away from the rest of the pile and down to the shoreline. Now if he could just find branches to fit between the layers of the pallet, he could add the buoyancy he'd need to support the Stone.

He gathered several pieces of barkless gray wood and worked as many as he could fit between the top and bottom layers of the pallet. When he was finished, he pushed it into the water to see how well it would float. It floated, but not well enough to support the weight he would need it to. So he pulled it ashore and headed back to the pile for some larger pieces.

It was probably about six a.m. when he dragged the large limbs down to shore. He didn't want the sun to dry everything up before he'd moved the Stone down the hillside. So Jevic headed back to the cairn and jumped into the hole to retrieve his bag and staff. With all of his running around, he'd forgotten to keep it as close as he should and held it for a few seconds to be sure he was alone. As he climbed out of the hollow for the last time, he spotted a small white stone in the dirt near the opening and picked it up. It looked like a little piece of white marble. Jevic smiled as he walked to the cairn and placed the pebble on the very top. This time the mound of stones did not pull at his medallion. He'd already found what his heart desired.

The entire hillside was slick, making the descent nearly effortless as he pushed the Stone down the slope. By the time he reached the bottom, his knees were scraped and bruised, but he didn't care. He left it on the bank, just above the shoreline, where he could slide it onto the raft when it was ready.

It took some time for him to tie two larger limbs to the underside of the pallet. Fishing line was all he had to secure the second log after using his pack straps for the first.

Jevic was a decent swimmer and was keeping an eye on the

depth of the water as he worked. The rocks he'd walked on to get there were only a couple of feet under the surface now. The problem was going to be crossing the deeper water between those rocks where he had no footing and would have to push the raft across the current while he swam.

As he moved the raft beneath the Stone on the bank, he realized how the rock stood out like a beacon in the daylight. What could he cover it with? He took his muddy sweatshirt over to the water to rinse it off and stretched it out on top of the pallet before climbing up behind the Stone on the bank. His heart beat a little faster as he carefully pushed the sacred treasure onto its raft. It fell into place as if it were finally giving the young Seer a little cooperation. Then he stretched the wet hoodie to its limit and zipped it closed around the spirits' treasure.

After tossing his backpack and staff onto the raft, Jevic shoved it into the shallow water near the shore. "Well, here we go," Jevic breathed, as he grabbed the empty sleeves of the shirt and dragged the raft further out into the river.

The weight of the Stone submerged the top of the pallet a couple of inches below the surface, but he thought it would be able to float well enough to reach the river bank. He'd walked diagonally from the bank to get there but decided to cut straight across this time, taking the shortest route possible. Although he wasn't at all familiar with the rocks in this direction, it really didn't matter—everything was different now.

The cloud of mud that was washing off of his clothes as he waded in made it difficult to see anything beneath the surface of the running water. The river was freezing, but at least he'd be cleaner when he reached the bank. He chose his steps wisely as he walked across a flat bed of rock where the water was only up to his knees. The arms of the sweatshirt now stretched four feet between the raft and the young man, and he held onto them tightly as he towed his precious cargo straight across the current.

About halfway across the 150 foot span, Jevic ran out of rock. He stood at the edge of a deep pool. It didn't seem to have much of a current, but he was afraid the weight of the raft might be too much for him to control without having his feet on the ground. He gave the raft a push and backtracked to where he could see a shallower route.

It was harder walking against the full current but it was definitely easier to maneuver the raft with his feet on the riverbed. The shoreline was only about fifty feet away when he met another dead end. How wide was the dark pool in front of him this time? He couldn't tell. But he wasn't very far from the bank, so how deep could it be?

With exhaustion and hunger wearing him down, Jevic decided to swim from there rather than backtrack again. He moved the raft in front of him so he could push it through the water. Launching himself off of the rock he'd been standing on, he propelled the pallet across the dark pool. As he swam, his eyes were focused down into the river in search of his next foothold. So it took him completely by surprise when he looked up and realized he was drifting with the current.

The river was carrying the raft downstream, while Jevic kicked like a mule to steer it back toward the bank. He looked over his shoulder just in time to avoid being crushed between the raft and a large boulder standing out of the water. As he passed around the side of the granite monster, the current picked up and he went under. When he came up, the raft was passing alongside of him. He grabbed for the sleeves and managed to catch one. Now both he and the raft were rolling with the current as Jevic's feet searched desperately for something solid beneath them.

Was he moving faster? He and the raft passed between a pair of giant rocks, and he was dragged under for a second time when the current surged around them. As the island appeared to be moving closer, all Jevic could think of were the waterfalls waiting downstream.

He swam to the side of the raft so he could see what lay ahead. Another set of granite giants were coming up fast. Snatching the hawthorn staff from beside the Stone, he held it horizontally just beneath the surface and wedged it between the two boulders. The raft banged against it and bounced off to the side of the boulder that was closer to shore. Jevic tossed his staff back onto the pallet and wrapped the sleeves around his wrist.

As the current fought to take the raft from him, he fought back, hanging onto the boulder closest to shore as an anchor. Terrified and breathless, Jevic reeled the Stone in little by little until he'd wedged himself between it and the boulder. The rapidly moving current was driving the raft against his chest, pinning him to the rock like a relentless bully. His strength was gone and his lungs felt as though they were about to explode. It was just like his dream—the Stone was going to be the death of him.

As his strength dwindled, the pallet pressed harder against his chest. He had nothing left to hold it back. Was this how it was all going to end?

If I let it go, I can probably still make it to shore, he reasoned. But he couldn't let go. There was much more at stake here than his life. He felt himself moving gradually around the side of the boulder. Fearing the inevitable, that moment the current would finally tear him away and pull him down again, Jevic reached out and pressed his fingers into their impressions on the top of his hawthorn staff.

"We gave it our best shot," he whispered.

"Jev!" he heard Brent's voice calling out to him from very far away.

You're hearing things, he told himself.

"Jevic, hang on!" his friend's voice called again.

He moved along the side of the raft so he could see around it to the riverbank. Brent was really there, standing on the shoreline waving his arms in the air over his head.

"I'll throw you a rope," he shouted, and then he disappeared into the bushes.

Jevic wondered if he was hallucinating. I can't just wait here until I get washed away, he told himself. He summoned all the strength he had left, turned toward the shore and kicked off of the boulder in a desperate attempt to force the raft to land.

Then, Brent called to him again. "Jev, catch the rope!"

Jevic shook the curls out of his eyes and watched the rope fall into the water about ten feet short of where he was.

"Hang on, I'll try again," Brent shouted as he frantically reeled the rope back in.

How much longer can I possibly hold on, Jevic asked himself?

"Hurry, Brent!" he shouted.

Brent ran out into the water up to his hips and threw the rope again. It landed only a couple of feet away. Jevic reached out with his staff and pulled the end of the rope to where he could reach it. He slipped the loop tied at the end over his head and under his arms.

"Okay!" he yelled, waving his hand in the air.

Brent wrapped the rope behind his waist and started backing out of the river. The slack tightened, and Jevic could feel himself moving slowly toward the shoreline. When Brent was back on solid ground and able to pull harder, Jevic was suddenly whipped around the back side of the raft, which was now barely resting against the back side of the boulder.

"Wait! Wait!" he yelled, reaching for the sweatshirt sleeves dangling off the side of the pallet. He pulled desperately against Brent at the other end of the rope. He had to get to the Stone before the current did!

"Jev, what are you doing?" Brent hollered. "Let it go! Whatever it is, let it go!"

"I can't!" Jevic shouted back. His hand closed with the cuff of the sleeve inside of it, and he wrapped it around his left wrist while holding onto the rope with his other hand.

Brent shook his head in disbelief. He planted his feet securely on the stony shoreline, and pulled with all of his might to haul his friend and the raft he refused to leave behind out of the dangerous current and into more shallow water.

Jevic's feet stumbled upon a solid rock ledge and he maneuvered the raft safely between the shore and where he stood in slow-running water up to his waist as he tried to catch his breath.

Brent came splashing up in front of him. "What the hell are you trying to do, get yourself killed?" he shouted angrily.

"Some things are worth dying for," Jevic said with a drained smile.

Brent looked at the square block wrapped in a gold Timberland sweatshirt and shook his head. "That's worth dying for? What the heck is it?" he asked.

Jevic stared at the Stone and thought about how he should answer that question. He knew he'd need his friend's help getting this thing back home and didn't know how much of the truth he could share. As he looked at the guy who'd just saved his life, an intense wave of paranoia took hold of him. What if this wasn't Brent? How convenient that someone showed up just when he needed help. He had to make sure it was really him.

"Do you remember that thing I gave you to hold on to for me?" Jevic asked.

Brent looked totally confused as Jevic held his breath and waited for a response.

"What? Now? You're freakin kidding me, right?" Brent scolded.

Jevic just stared and waited desperately for the proof he needed.

"What an idiot!" Brent mumbled as he reached into his pocket and whipped out a soaking wet wallet. He flipped angrily through the plastic photo sleeves to the one holding half of a dollar bill and held it out to show Jevic. "Here," he snapped, "Sorry, if it's a little wet."

Jevic smiled and shook his head hard from side to side, splashing water into his friend's face.

"Hey!" Brent yelled.

"Thanks...for not listening to me," Jevic told him. "Although, I pretty much had things under control."

Brent raised a brow. "That's what you call under control?" he challenged. "I don't know who's crazier...you, or me for hanging out with you."

Without another word, they each grabbed a sleeve and

towed the raft safely to shore. Jevic sat down on the edge of the pallet while Brent coiled his rope.

"Thanks, Brent," Jevic said after catching his breath. "I wish I could tell you what's going on."

Brent sat down beside him. "If you can't, I'm sure you have a good reason. I'm just glad you're okay."

Jevic threw his arm around Brent's shoulder. "Someday I'll tell you everything…and then you'll really think I'm nuts," he told him with a smile.

Jevic wondered what would he have done if Brent hadn't shown up? Then he said quietly, "I really love you, bro."

Brent threw his arm around Jevic's trembling, cold shoulders and gave him pat. "I love you too, Jev," he answered.

They sat quietly for a minute, watching the river flow past, both of them happy to still have the other.

Brent broke the silence when he asked, "So this sweatshirt isn't illegal or anything, right?"

"No, but it's pretty heavy stuff though," Jevic told him.

Brent nodded. "And where do you plan to take it?" he asked.

Jevic's heart sank when he realized his challenge wasn't over yet. "To my woods," he answered heavily.

Brent responded with a toothy grin. "Then I guess it's a good thing I brought my brother's quad with me, isn't it?"

Jevic popped off of the raft like a champagne cork. "No kidding?" he asked.

Brent ran into the bushes, and Jevic heard the engine start up. Without saying another word, Brent backed the quad up close to the raft and they struggled to lift the Stone onto the rack on back of the four-wheeler. It was no easy task. But where there's a will, there's a way. After several minutes, they had it loaded and securely tied on with bungee cords.

Jevic retrieved the nylon straps from the raft and reattached them to his pack. They slipped on their helmets and rode the quad up the path to the church parking lot and turned onto the road toward home. He would have to come back later for his bike, but he didn't mind. All he wanted to do was get the Stone safely into his woods as quickly as possible before anyone saw him. It wasn't illegal, but it would definitely raise plenty of unwanted questions if they were caught with it.

Riding in the ditch alongside the main road was slow-going with the weight they were hauling. Jevic breathed a bit easier when they turned onto the trail through his woods and climbed up the hill parallel to the West Brook.

The trees looked happy to see him, even on the back of the annoying machine they were riding. He held his breath as they passed the dead oak with its visibly charred bark and watched over his shoulder for a while to be sure they weren't followed.

He directed Brent to the Triad where he asked him to back up as close as he could to the oak tree. They pushed the sweatshirt gently from the rack onto the slope of the hillside at Osred's feet.

"Now what?" Brent asked.

"Now…I guess I'm better off on my own again," Jevic said with a guilty, almost painful smile.

"Are you sure?" Brent questioned.

"Yeah. I'll call you later," Jevic said. "Thanks for everything, Brent."

"That's what friends are for." Brent said as he closed the other helmet in a storage compartment. "Later, dude!" he said with a smirk. Then he rode off over the hill leaving Jevic standing alone before the Triad. The young Seer was wet, dirty and completely exhausted as he lifted his eyes toward the spirit face of the oak.

Osred looked at the young human with hopeful anticipation.

Jevic pulled the medallion out from under his shirt. There was no time for protocol. "Osred, can you please let me pass?" he asked. "I have a very important delivery to make."

"You've done it, haven't you?" Osred murmured, and then, as if he already knew the answer, a tear rolled down the side of his long, crooked nose.

The Seer nodded with a weary smile. As the trees cheered

and praised him, the ground rumbled and the great oak rose up from the forest floor revealing the light from the Otherworld within.

Jevic looked around nervously and asked, "Please, don't waste any time closing this behind me." Then he grabbed the sleeves of the sweatshirt and pulled on the heavy stone with what little strength he had left. He'd moved it halfway through the doorway when he felt a hand on his shoulder. He froze. He'd come so far. Jevic reluctantly turned his gaze toward his left shoulder and recognized the fingerless leather glove on Aaron's hand.

"Can I help you with that?" the prince asked.

Jevic spun around and saw the prince standing beside him. It felt as though a huge weight had been lifted from his shoulders.

"Yes!" his voice cracked. The young man extended his hand, and Aaron's locked solidly around it. Then he pulled the boy's head against his chest in a powerful embrace.

"I've never been so proud of anyone," Aaron whispered with tears glistening in his dark eyes.

But Jevic was still anxious and would be until the Stone was safely inside. "How about that help?" he said with an exhausted grin.

Together they dragged the sacred Stone of Destiny by the very, very long sleeves of its Timberland hoodie into the corridor beneath the oak. And, as requested, Osred wasted no time closing the hill with them safely inside.

19 ~ THE HOMECOMING ~

By the time the doorway beneath the oak was closed, the news of the Stone's return had already spread throughout the Seelie Kingdom and a tremendous celebration had commenced. Jubilant music echoed up through the corridor where Aaron stared in utter amazement at the young man beside him.

"You look like you've had quite a battle, young warrior," he said.

"Yeah, but I won!" Jevic told him. He was worn out, but beaming. "I never could have done it without my friend's help. In fact, I probably would have..." he stopped. It all seemed so unreal to him now, like a nightmare still too fresh to rationalize.

"Want to see it?" Jevic asked excitedly.

"You know I do!" Aaron told him.

Jevic threw himself onto his knees to unzip the sweatshirt. It was then that he recognized the similarity between the Timberland logo and the tree of life he wore around his neck. He noticed the spot of pine sap beside the zipper that had been there since the day he and Brent started building their cabin—the day he'd first seen the pine's face and then so many others. All that he'd been through had led to this moment, and

Jevic rather unceremoniously peeled the gold cloth away from the Stone.

Prince Aaron was overwhelmed and dropped to the ground beside him. The Stone of Destiny was the cornerstone of his entire world; taken from those who loved it and coveted for its power by those who did not in the world above. But it was finally here, back in the realm of the spirits, where their mystical Stone belonged. As incredible as it was to believe, the first of the sacred Sidhe treasures had finally come home.

Jevic saw the prince's face and sat back on his heels, content in knowing he had accomplished something amazingly important for Aaron and his people.

"Touch it," the young Seer urged.

Aaron looked up from the Stone to the young man beside him. To lay his hand on this rock would be his submission to its judgment. This magnificent stone had the power to proclaim him the next ruler of his father's kingdom. It also had the power to deny him that throne by remaining silent upon his touch. His eyes gazed upon the breathtaking tree carved into the marble, and like Jevic, he too could feel the energy it possessed without laying a hand on it.

"What are you waiting for?" Jevic asked. "You don't think I went through all of that trouble just so you could look at it, do you?"

Aaron smiled and shook his head. "You're right. It's time for me to face my own destiny," he said.

Jevic sat perfectly still as the prince bowed his head and extended his right hand over the Stone. He hesitated for a moment to steal a deep breath, and then he laid his hand upon it.

An astonishing burst of light flooded the corridor. Jevic closed his eyes to the blinding radiance that surrounded him but opened them wide when next a phenomenal roar erupted from the Stone. It rolled like thunder through the corridor to the kingdom below. The voice of the Stone was beyond anything he could have imagined. It moved through him like a magnificent wave of electricity. It shook the walls around them and the ground beneath their knees.

Aaron lifted his head, and Jevic looked upon the face of a man charged with the energy of the great Stone. He glowed with strength and belief in his own destiny as he smiled at his young friend, the young man who had changed the course of history.

"Jevic, thank you," Aaron said. Those three words were the most sincere, meaningful words Jevic had ever been given by another.

"It was an honor, King Aaron," he replied with a smile that stretched from ear to ear.

On the other side of the great wall that divided the Seelie from the Unseelie Court, the brilliant flash of light and the mighty roar of the Stone brought thousands of Unseelie troops to their knees. The blinding light of truth pierced their unblessed eyes, and the undeniable voice of the Stone forced them to cover their ears, for the truth was too hard to hear.

King Magnus rolled off of his throne and cried out in agony. Then, pulling himself to his knees, he raised his fists into the air and screamed defiantly at the top of his lungs, but not a single word was audible over the Stone's roar. The voice of destiny had spoken.

When Aaron removed his hand, the Stone fell silent. He gave the young man beside him another powerful hug. "Anything," he said, "If there is ever anything I can do for you, Jevic, please ask."

"Well, there is one thing," Jevic said.

Aaron laughed, "That was quick."

"Help me carry this to your father?"

"It will be my pleasure," Aaron answered.

With one of them on either side, they reached down and lifted the Stone as if it were as light as a feather. Jevic didn't know how it was possible for the load he'd struggled with to have been lightened so suddenly, but he was sure that it had something to do with the power of this incredible place, the power of the Stone itself, and the powerful friendship he'd forged with the prince.

As long as Aaron was in contact with the Stone, it continued to sound its tremendous approval of the man destined for the throne. Jevic hoped Alicia could even hear the roar back inside their stone house.

The treasure bearers glowed with pride as they stepped out of the corridor and walked across the courtyard carrying the marvelous gift to the king.

Thousands of Sidhe and other beings of the fairy realm who'd gathered around the courtyard were cheering and dancing in celebration as they watched their precious treasure returning home. There were tiny spirits the size of fireflies, as well as pixies, wood elves, trolls, brownies, and the tall, slender Sidhe. All sizes, colors and shapes of beings that dwelled in this breathtaking realm were there to greet their beloved Stone with jubilation. Although Jevic could not hear them over the roar, he could feel their joy and was overwhelmed with pride for the part he'd played in its return.

The royal guard met them at the steps and escorted them not only into the palace but all the way to the king's bed chamber; at which point, they lined the hallway outside of the heavy door as the prince and the young human carried the Stone inside.

Queen Nia greeted them with teary-eyes and a beautiful smile. If possible, the Stone seemed to roar even louder as they approached the king. The heavy, velvet drapes that encircled his majesty's bed rippled with the force of the roar as it moved the air like a fierce wind.

As King Ronan's eyes gazed at the marble treasure, he remembered the day the Stone had roared for him the way it now did for his son. A bittersweet smile embraced the old monarch's face, for the dreams he had for his kingdom were at last being fulfilled.

Aaron gave Jevic a nod, and he carried the stone up the platform by himself, setting it down on a red velvet stool beside his father's bed. The instant he removed his hands, the Stone fell silent again. It was brilliant, gleaming like a block of new-fallen snow, the vibration having cleaned every speck of dirt from its surface.

As Aaron knelt beside the stool, his father reached out and laid a hand on top of his head. "The Stone has chosen well," King Ronan said. "Do you accept this destiny, my son?"

"I do, Sire," Prince Aaron replied.

"Very well, the coronation will take place tomorrow morning," the king announced.

Jevic smiled proudly, enjoying the fruits of his labor, as King Ronan kissed the top of Aaron's head. But when he heard the king call out, "Jevic!" he jumped with surprise.

Suddenly aware of his mud-stained clothes, the young man ran his fingers through his hair as he walked quickly up the steps. "Your Highness," he answered, kneeling on the left side of the Stone opposite Aaron.

The king smiled warmly as he looked down at the young man before him. "Jevic, I hope you realize what you have done," he said solemnly. "You did not have to answer the call. You chose to, and there is nothing more powerful than the free will of a human spirit. We are blessed by your presence here and this world will be forever in your debt."

Jevic didn't really know what to say, except, "I'm happy that I could help, Sire. I could not have done it without my friends though," he added, feeling quite guilty for having lied to them all.

"I am honored to know you, Jevic O'Connor," said King Ronan. Then, following a brief moment of silence, he asked, "Aaron, may I borrow your sword?"

The prince rose immediately to his feet. "Yes, Father," he replied as he slipped the golden blade from its scabbard and presented it to the king.

Ronan grasped the hilt and lowered the blade to rest on Jevic's right shoulder. The boy's eyes opened wide in disbelief as he heard the Seelie King say, "You unselfishly assumed the burden of my kingdom as your own. You demonstrated honor, courage and the undying light of human spirit. Those of this world will forever remember your name Sir Jevic O'Connor, Knight of the Seelie Court."

Jevic was breathless. As Ronan lifted the blade and tapped his other shoulder, the boy bit his lip and swallowed hard. "Thank you, Sire," he whispered humbly. When the king nodded to his son, Aaron returned the blade to its scabbard.

"I never doubted you, Jevic," King Ronan informed him. "You have the heart of your great-grandfather. He was a very good man." Then, the king lay back on his pillow and closed his eyes.

Jevic watched the Seelie King resting peacefully. He wished he'd gotten to know him better. Perhaps it was his great-grandfather whose path was connected with Ronan's, as his now was with Aaron's. Overwhelmed and briefly lost in his own thoughts, Jevic suddenly realized he was still kneeling beside the king's bed. He found his feet and joined Aaron who was waiting by the door.

"I was just thinking about stuff," Jevic said, feeling a little awkward for his momentary drift from reality. Reality, what was that anyway? He was still distracted when his stomach growled loudly, and the prince laughed.

"I think it's about time we get you dry clothes and something to eat, Sir Jevic," Aaron said with a wink.

"Sir Jevic," the young knight whispered, holding his head high and puffing up his chest. Then he exhaled heavily, blowing the curls off of his forehead, "I sure hope I can live up to that."

Aaron gave him a solid pat on the back. "You already have," he said.

While the celebration in the Seelie Court geared up for the coronation, Jevic had something to eat and got some well-deserved sleep. Aaron asked him to stay for the coronation and assured the young knight that he'd return home within an hour or so of when he'd entered the hill. Although it seemed hard to believe, he trusted the prince's word and agreed to stay.

After eating his fill, Jevic could barely keep his eyes open. While telling Aaron all about the challenges he'd faced on the island, he drifted off to sleep mid-sentence while lying on Prince Jevic's bed.

Early the next morning, he washed and dressed in some of Aaron's old clothes; a long white tunic that buttoned up the front with billowing sleeves and a pair of light brown pants that fit much too tightly for his preference. Yet in this place, they suited him perfectly and made him feel like a real part of this wonderful spirit world. As he adjusted a wide brown belt on the outside of his tunic, an unsettling thought came over him. Now that the Stone was back where it belonged, would this be his last visit here? His contemplation was interrupted by an unexpected knock on the door.

"Come in," he called, and Aaron entered the room.

"A perfect fit," the prince commented. "You look like you belong here."

"I feel like I do," Jevic admitted. "I'm sure going to miss it."

Aaron sat in the plush green chair in the corner. "What do you mean?" he asked.

"Well, I did what I was supposed to do, so…" the boy stopped short of completing his thought and looked down as he fiddled with his belt.

"So what?" Aaron asked. "So you want nothing more to do with us?"

"No! I just figured I'm no longer needed here now that the Stone is back where it belongs," Jevic mumbled.

Aaron laughed loudly. "Good friends are always needed, and you will always be welcome here, Jevic."

The young man looked at the prince leaning forward in his chair with his elbows on his knees.

"Really?" he asked.

"Really," Aaron answered with a smirk. "This room has been empty since my uncle passed to the heavens. I think he'd be happy to know it's yours now."

Jevic's mouth dropped wide open and a single word fell out of it. "Mine?" He couldn't believe it. He could still be a part of all this. "I'll still be able to see and hear the spirits too?" he quizzed.

"Those are your gifts," Aaron answered, leaning back into

the chair.

"And the medallion?" Jevic asked reluctantly while looking down at the Tree of Life resting against his chest. He felt an incredible emptiness with the mere thought of losing it.

"It's yours. My father meant for you to keep it," Aaron assured him.

"Awesome!" the boy burst with excitement. "So, I can still come here and see you?"

"Jevic, you're the little brother I never had. Please, consider this your home," the prince told him.

The young man breathed a sigh of relief. "This is great! I couldn't imagine having to leave and not being able come back."

It was all too good to be true until Jevic remembered his family and friends. When he realized he'd have to keep lying to them, his heart sank. Just a couple of weeks ago, he was an ordinary kid.

Jevic looked at the soon-to-be king sitting in front of him and smiled. "Thanks for believing in me, and for being there when I needed you," he said.

Aaron smiled warmly at the boy who'd stepped right out of a fairy tale that he'd believed in since he was a child. "That's what brothers do, Jevic," he told him.

20 ~ NEW BEGINNINGS ~

Garlands of beautiful flowers, which hung in the air with no visible means of support, decorated the courtyard. The tinkling of thousands of tiny bells, one in each fairy's hand, filled the air as the king and queen approached their thrones.

Jevic stood at the bottom of the steps, surprised to see King Ronan walking arm in arm with Queen Nia from the palace. When the royal couple took their seats, the air fell silent.

Jevic was startled by the blast of three long trumpets sounding a salute as Prince Aaron crossed the mosaic floor amidst a shower of white rose petals. For the first time since Jevic had known him, the prince was not dressed in his dark leather armor but in pure white. His pants and matching tunic shimmered with light and the hilt of his golden sword rested on top of a solid gold scabbard instead of the black leather one he usually wore. A beautiful white cape, reaching mid-calf, flowed behind him as Aaron passed Jevic with a wink and ascended the steps toward the thrones.

When the Seelie Court's newest knight recognized the Tree of Life embroidered in gold on the back of the prince's cape, he felt a lump tighten in his throat. And as Aaron's right knee hit the floor, the entire kingdom waited in silence for King

Ronan to speak.

"We often hear the things that we from this realm can do referred to as magic by those of the physical world above. For hundreds of years, despite all of our powerful gifts, we were unable to retrieve the Stone of Destiny from those who had taken it from us," the king said in a weak but confident voice. "Yesterday, when a young man accomplished what no one else could for over a thousand years, we witnessed the extraordinary power of human magic. Let this be an example to each of us, and to all of mankind, that anything is possible if we believe it to be."

The king looked at the young human standing near the front of the crowd at the bottom of the great steps and said, "Sir Jevic of the Seelie Court, you have my kingdom's deepest gratitude and our eternal friendship."

The crowd exploded with cheers and the sound of fairy bells rang blissfully through the air. Jevic smiled at King Ronan, Queen Nia and Aaron, who looked proudly over his shoulder at him. The young man was overwhelmed as the cheers continued even after he had turned and humbly waved at the crowd around him. The king finally raised his hand to silence the masses, for which Jevic was incredibly grateful.

Then Ronan turned to his son. "Prince Aaron, do you accept the throne and the responsibility it holds to the Sidhe?" he asked.

"I do, your Highness," the prince replied.

"Do you vow to protect this kingdom and preserve its God-given lands, its values, and its people from all those who would oppose them, no matter what the cost?"

"I do, your Highness," the prince replied.

"Are you prepared to be judged worthy by the great Stone of Destiny?"

"I am, your Highness," the prince replied again.

"Bring the Stone," the king ordered.

Jevic noticed a third throne to the left of King Ronan as four guards carried the Stone past on a platform draped in white cloth. As they lowered it from their shoulders to place it on the floor between the king and prince, there were audible gasps from the crowd. Jevic could feel the excitement building around him as many of those present got their first glimpse of the treasured relic.

"Stone of Destiny," the king's voice boomed with surprising volume. "We seek your approval. Does Prince Aaron have your blessing to take my throne and rule the Kingdom of the Sidhe?" Ronan nodded to the prince, and Aaron laid his right hand on the sacred Stone before the entire kingdom.

Again, there was a tremendous flash of blinding light as the Stone expressed a phenomenal roar of approval that rolled like thunder over the courtyard and throughout the entire realm. The crowd also expressed its unanimous approval, but the voice of the great Stone drowned them out. The garlands of flowers swung back and forth overhead, and the ground quaked. When Aaron lifted his hand from the magnificent stone, it fell silent, but the crowd continued to rejoice.

"I believe we have the Stone's approval," King Ronan said with a smile. "And I believe the people of the Seelie Kingdom are happy with its decision."

The crowd cheered even louder than before, and he raised a tired hand to silence them again. "It has been a great honor to serve you good people. Please show my son the love that you have shown me." Then King Ronan lifted the golden crown from his own head and placed it gently upon his son's with the words, "I crown thee, King Aaron of the Sidhe!"

Jevic was thoroughly surprised by the renewed energy in King Ronan and wondered if the Stone may have blessed him with its magic.

Aaron rose to his feet and his father kissed him on one cheek and then the other, after which Aaron turned to face his people for the first time as their ruler. At that moment, the air erupted with such jubilant celebration that it may even have rivaled the roar of the Stone.

Jevic looked around in awe as the Seelie people sang and cheered, "Long live King Aaron! Long live the king!" He was completely unaware of Aaron's approach until he felt a hand rest upon his shoulder. The young man beamed with pride as the king who called him brother lead him to the top of the platform amidst a shower of rainbow colored flowers. Tiny fairies shot into the air like fireworks, shifting and dancing in a kaleidoscope of color over the crowd.

Aaron put his arm across the boy's shoulders. "My kingdom thanks you, Sir Jevic. All of this has happened because of you," he told him.

"…and my friends," Jevic added. Too bad they'll never know what they've done, he thought.

It was hard for the young man to leave the spirit realm that day, but he had other promises to keep, like calling Brent, who he wished more than anyone could understand how important a role he'd played in all that had happened.

Even more amazing was the fact that when Brent came by later that afternoon, he never once asked about the mysterious object he'd helped carry home. The two of them just worked on the cabin, without sinking a single nail into the old pine tree that cradled them safely in its branches every night that summer as they slept out in those magical woods.

It was just about one year later that Jevic and Brent were walking to the cabin with their sleeping bags for the first campout of the summer. They were both sixteen now and a little taller. Despite all of the time Jevic had spent at his other home during the past year, he and Brent had grown even closer than they ever were before.

Jevic smiled at the friendly pine spirit as he approached. And as he climbed up into the cabin and tossed his sleeping bag inside, he heard Brent give a little shout from the outside.

"Ouch! What was that?"

Jevic poked his head out the door and saw him standing beside the ladder rubbing the back of his calf.

"What's wrong?" he asked.

"I got stung or something," Brent answered rather indifferently. But when he looked up from his leg and noticed a little man leaning against the tree beside him, he shrieked. Dropping his sleeping bag and scrambling up the ladder, Brent flew past Jevic into the cabin.

"Jev, there's something out there!" he squeaked, his eyes wide with fear.

Jevic looked down to see Aaron, in his wood elf guise, near the base of the tree, and his expression twisted with confusion. He turned back toward Brent, and asked, "What are you talking about?"

"It's some kind of...little person!" Brent shouted excitedly. "Can't you see him?"

Jevic looked from Brent to the wood elf and back again. "You can see him?" Jevic asked in disbelief.

"Can't you?" Brent shouted frantically.

Jevic poked his head out the door and gave Aaron a scrutinizing glare. The elf raised his eyebrows and looked away nonchalantly.

"You didn't?" Jevic shouted at the little man. "Did you?"

"Maybe just a little poke," Aaron replied with a smirk.

"No way! No way!" Jevic shouted excitedly. "Why would you do that?"

"I need your help again, and you will need him," the small king replied, as he slipped the golden sword back into place at his side. "I want to know you'll have someone there you can trust."

Jevic backed slowly into the doorway. He leaned against the wall beside the opening and stared at his best friend pressed into the opposite corner. It couldn't be. This was too incredible to believe.

"Jev, don't mess with me," Brent demanded. "Were you just talking to that little guy? You can see him, can't you?" He was desperate for an explanation and couldn't understand why his friend was so calm under the circumstances. Suddenly Brent's eyes shimmered with realization, and he asked, "You know that guy, don't you?"

Jevic raked his curls back, revealing an incredible glow of excitement on his face.

"Yes, Brent. I know him," he admitted, but as he struggled for a way to explain, the full-sized Aaron appeared beside him in the doorway.

Brent pressed himself deeper into the far corner of the small cabin. "How the hell did he do that?" he squealed.

"Brent, it's okay. I promise," Jevic reassured. Then with a pat on the king's shoulder, he introduced, "This is my very, very good friend, Aaron."

Brent's face screwed up like he'd lost all sense of reality, and Jevic knew exactly how he felt. Only time could help that. Right now, the young knight was about to explode with excitement. Everything was going to be different from this point forward. Everything was going to be so much better.

Jevic flashed his best friend a brilliant smile and said, "Now I can tell you everything!"

ABOUT THE AUTHOR

Her fascination with the spirit realm and connection to the wild places of the earth inspired Lisa Popp to write the Jevic O'Connor series. Having a natural flair for design, Lisa also created the cover art, which features her own interpretation of the Tree of Life. When not writing, this author can be found hiking, camping and kayaking with her husband and family.